FIRST CHRISTMAS

D. RAVEN

TABLE OF CONTENTS

BLURB

Rebecca Wareman and Lucas Marshall have found
their happily ever after.

Or have they?
Rebecca finds herself finally free from running.
Her daughter is safe and thriving.
The monster has been slayed.
But what happens when trauma catches up with her
and she's left alone with her thoughts?

Lucas has everything he's ever wanted.
A beautiful, strong fiancée.
A spunky, playful daughter.
Will he be able to save Becks from herself so that
their happily ever can last?

To everyone who knows real relationships
take work and fight for them daily.

PLAYLIST

"The Reason" by Hoobastank

"Silver Bells" by Dean Martin

"Carol of the Bells" by Pentatonix *(Becks' Favorite Christmas song)*

"Can't Help Falling in Love" by Elvis Presley

"Fix You" by Coldplay

"Chasing Cars" by Snow Patrol *(Lucas and Becks' song)*

"We Wish You A Merry Christmas" by Weezer *(Lucas' Favorite Christmas song)*

"Last Christmas" by Taylor Swift *(Nat's Favorite Christmas song)*

"You're a Mean One, Mr. Grinch" by Tyler, the Creator *(Because there's nothing D. Raven loves more than The Grinch at Christmas)*

NOTE FROM THE AUTHOR

CHAPTER ONE

BECKS

"Natasha!"

I dropped my straightener on the vanity's top and sighed at the mess on Lucas' side. His toothbrush was rinsed, but laying two inches away from the holder and the toothpaste was uncapped beside it. His hair brush was inside the sink, up on its end, carelessly tossed when he'd left for his pre-sunrise start of shift this morning. Beard hair was everywhere from where he'd obviously trimmed it.

Lucas and I had been together for a while now, engaged to be married, and quickly coming up on our first Christmas living under one roof. I met my dark brown eyes in the mirror and shook my head. It's been more of an adjustment than I anticipated. I'd spent so long being lonely, that now, living with another adult, has proven to be more of a challenge. I wasn't prepared.

Sure, I'd had Nat cohabitating with me all these years but this was different. I had been in an abusive marriage thirteen years ago and left the moment I found out about her. Having a child was different than this, you taught them what to do and enforced it. I'd always been organized. Everything had its place and was labeled. I didn't think I was some Type A bitch, but man, being engaged and living with someone was sure showing me a lot about myself.

I loved my fiancé. He quite literally saved me from a lifetime of loneliness and gave my daughter the father figure she had always been missing in her life. He was six-feet-six-inches of husky, tattooed, close-cut-bearded sexiness. But the man was a slob. Okay. . .maybe I was being a little dramatic when I said slob. He was a little messy. He was always in such a rush that he didn't leave enough time to clean up after himself.

I, on the other hand, was used to planning extra time to make sure I could put things back where they went.

"Natasha!" I yelled again at the lack of response, "We're going to be late!"

I turned the straightener off and laid it on the hot mat on my tidy side of the sink. I stopped to give Lucas' area another moment of serious side eye. I ironically didn't have time to clean up after him today.

I knew it shouldn't bother me this much. No one came into our private bathroom unless it was an emergency, no guests would see it, but I'd always liked things neat and tidy. My ex-husband had lived like an actual slob and been a borderline hoarder. He hadn't let me clean and I'd often be in trouble if I broke and did so.

When I was finally free of him, I'd let myself clean and organize to my heart's content. I was even able to earn a living as a professional organizer. The fact that half of my bathroom looked like this was bothering me more than the typical person. I'd developed some major obsessive-compulsive tendencies over the years that I used to help when my anxiety manifested. The therapist I was seeing currently was helping me work through these things.

I walked down the hall to the bottom of the stairs, and looked up for any sign of life from my daughter. Her dark head finally came into view at the top. She was still in her pajamas.

"What are you doing?" I asked. "We have to be at the school in thirty minutes. This is your last week before Christmas break."

I'd taken the next few weeks off until after the New Year to spend time with Nat. I'd never been able to do it before as a single mother. Lucas was adamant I do it this year. As I looked at my thirteen year old she wrapped her arms around herself. I smiled softly at her choice of pajamas. She was wearing sleep shorts that matched one of Lucas' police tee shirts, and her hair was rumpled. Her light blue eyes met my own and I noticed she looked flushed.

"I don't feel good," she mumbled with a soft groan.

"Shit," I muttered under my breath. This wasn't in the plan.

She turned to walk back down the upstairs hallway to her room.

I jogged up the stairs tucking my beach-waved, ebony hair behind my ears.

"Should've gone with the ponytail," I said to myself, grabbing a towel she'd left on the floor as I went.

Turning into Nat's room, I caught her ducking into her private bathroom, and immediately heard the tell-sign of vomiting.

"Fuck," I sighed softly, wiping my hands over my face. "Honey, are you okay?" I asked, knowing she'd get upset if I came in there to mother hen over her.

Gone were the days when she ran to me when she was sick. She informed me daily that she was a teenager now. I approached the bathroom doorway, giving her room a onceover. Her phone charger and phone were laying on the carpet by the nightstand. The carpet under her bed was somehow crooked, laying across the hardwood floor. Clothes were everywhere instead of in the hamper. Her fairy lights were on and television paused on some obscure movie she and Lexi had been watching the last time they were up here together.

I picked up the gym bag she used for volleyball and immediately held it away from me. I thought teenage boys were supposed to be the stinky ones. Turns out it was teenagers as a whole. Lucas was definitely rubbing off on her. I guess it looked like a typical thirteen year old's room, but it was getting bad.

I stopped and took a couple of deep breaths.

Now was not the time.

Usually my anxiety set off a cleaning and organizing mood and it was worse than usual today. I guess my special Christmas season anxiety was kicking in.

Nat came to the bathroom door, groaning and still looking pale. I placed my cool hand against her burning forehead.

"Oh, baby. Get in bed. I'm going to get the thermometer, you're burning up."

I turned on my heel after she nodded weakly at me and walked barefoot back down the hall and stairs. Opening the hallway closet, I swear to God my eye twitched. It too was an absolute disaster. I was starting to feel like a raving bitch. I took a deep breath and counted to ten. Moving around unfolded linens and towels, I found the sick basket.

I'd always had a tub, bucket, or basket with kleenex, a thermometer, and medications for any ailment ready to go. Being a single mom meant I had no time to hunt and gather these things sometimes. There was no one else to yell at to grab them when your toddler was projectile vomiting or pooping across the house. It had just stuck with me at this point. Balancing the basket on my plus-sized hip, I jogged back up the stairs and down the hall. I was relieved I hadn't put my hoodie on and was just wearing my leggings and soft, short-sleeved shirt.

Nat was already curled up in bed, burrowed under the blankets with her bathroom trash can beside her. Setting the sick basket on the bed, I grabbed the thermometer and moved her dark hair off her sweaty forehead. I scanned her temple and groaned at the one hundred and two degree temperature that greeted me.

"I think you've caught the flu."

Her best friend's family had been down with it the week before. It had made the rounds through the schools. My best friend Monica was the school receptionist and had warned me before it took her family out of commission. Lexi was Monica's daughter, and Nat's best friend.

I handed Nat some Tylenol and ducked into her bathroom to get her sink cup and fresh water. I ignored the toothpaste in the sink and hair ties strewn across the floor and vanity. Reaching over I shut off her hair straightener, noting to give her another safety lecture when she was feeling better. Walking back into her room I handed her the cup and gel caps she'd laid on the nightstand. Making sure she took them and was laying back down, I pulled my cell phone out and shot a text to my best friend.

> Nat has the bug.

Monica

Damn. I'd hoped she'd missed it.

Me too. She won't be in today, obviously.

Ah, the perks of being besties with the school receptionist meant I didn't have to hold to speak to someone.

Monica

I'll mark it down. Tell my love bug I hope she feels better soon.

I smiled. My best friend was the absolute best. She'd had a rough time of it the past few months. Losing her husband of over a decade in a tragic situation. A tragic situation that I still felt like was all my fault. It was something I was struggling with daily even though she constantly assured me she didn't hold it against me. I still woke up with night terrors about the entire situation. I couldn't imagine how she was coping with things and being left alone with her two daughters. I wondered when Lucas was going to grow weary of being woken up to me thrashing around or screaming.

Thanks, Mon. I love you.

Monica

I love you too.

I didn't feel like I deserved that love. Sighing I glanced at my daughter and saw she'd drifted off to sleep. Tip-toeing out of the room, I left the door ajar and called my fiancé.

"Hey, gorgeous," came his gravely, low voice as I held my phone to my ear.

"Hey, baby," I vaguely remembered him kissing my forehead and whispering he loved me before leaving at four o'clock a.m, "Natasha has the bug."

"Nooooo," he groaned, "Is she okay? Does she need anything? Do you need anything? What do I do?"

Laughing softly, I stepped into the kitchen and over to the coffee pot, pushing start. This would be his first illness with Natasha. I often forgot how over the top he could be with her. It was like she was his newborn baby. I had to keep reminding him that as a teenager she could use that against him.

"It's probably just the flu, Lucas. I've given her Tylenol and she's already back asleep. It kind of has to run its course, sweetheart. I was just letting you know I have to call in. I may have to make up the day I'm missing next week when I was supposed to be on vacation."

"Oh. Well that's okay."

That's okay? I thought to myself. He'd been on me for months to make sure I'd taken the week off for myself. I shook my head, brushing it off.

"Are you feeling okay?" I asked, watching the coffee drip and willing it to go faster. Caffeine was very important to me.

"I feel fine. Right as rain. I don't remember the last time I was sick," he assured me. I could hear the buzz of the station in the background and my heart clenched. I still expected to hear Monica's husband, Paul's voice in the background making some smartass remark, or grabbing the phone to talk to me, just to irritate Lucas.

"Yeah. Me neither. I've been pretty good about not catching anything Nat has had. Just a couple of colds."

I knocked on the wooden, cutting board counter of the

kitchen bar, just in case I'd jinxed myself.

"I'll see you around one o'clock this afternoon?" I asked.

"Yep. I'll stop by the cafe and bring home some of their chicken noodle soup for all of us. I'll get extra for Peanut."

My heart melted hearing this man's nickname for our daughter. He hadn't had a hand in making her but you couldn't tell she wasn't his. She was meant for him, just like I was. I rubbed my hand over my chest glancing around the airy kitchen. It could use some straightening as well.

"That sounds great. I'm going to call work and let them know. I love you."

"I love you too, sweetheart."

I sighed, pouring some sugar into the bottom of my coffee mug. I usually drank iced coffee, but the weather outside was gray and the forecast finally called for snow. It felt like a morning for hot coffee.

As I called into work and waited for the coffee to finish, I cleaned and straightened the kitchen. I at least had a day to clean up and organize the house I felt was in chaos. Even if it was going to end up right back to its current condition within a week.

A couple of hours later, I tip-toed into Nat's room to check on her. I'd managed to clean and organize the kitchen, the hall closet, and the bathroom I shared with Lucas. If Nat hadn't been sick, I'd have tackled her room too. It was the only other spot in the house that really needed it.

Laying my hand on her forehead gently, I breathed a sigh of

relief that she felt cooler, though still warm. This bug seemed to only last 24-48 hours. Monica had said Lacey and Lexi had only thrown up once or twice. It was the fever and exhaustion that had hit them all.

I sighed, thinking of my friend as I left the room again. Lucas and I had a very special Christmas present planned for her. It was our first Christmas as best friends, and her first holiday season without her husband. I winced as I thought about the past again. My therapist said to move on, but it was hard when there were so many reminders in my day to day life.

After thirteen years of running and fear, I'd met Lucas and Monica. They were the best things to ever happen to me outside of Natasha. Unfortunately, my ex-husband Clark, and his best friend, Larry had finally caught up with me. Things had gotten very dire and resulted in Paul losing his life.

Seeing me meet Lucas and starting to move on had been Clark's last straw. He and Larry had gone as far as to kidnap and torture me. When Paul had been the one to find me at the old house on the abandoned farm, Larry had overtaken him, and he'd been killed in action.

I took a shaky breath, standing at the top of the stairs. I closed my eyes, took a deep breath in for ten seconds, and counted out to ten slowly. My therapist was trying to teach me coping mechanisms that weren't as harmful and obsessively cleaning the same spot on the floor for fifteen minutes. They only helped sometimes.

If it wasn't bad enough that I had post-traumatic stress from an abusive relationship and marriage, now I had some from witnessing all that I had.

Watching Paul die in front of me had broken something inside of me. It was my fault. He'd still be here if I hadn't come to this town. Lucas had immediately insisted that I see a therapist that he knew through the force. He promised that he, and his Nan, were the only two that knew I was seeing one.

I didn't feel right telling Monica I was in therapy because it was her husband who had died. Yes, I'd been kidnapped and nearly killed, but I felt responsible for my best friend, my sister's, current heartache and pain. I felt like I'd stolen something from her and her girls.

Sighing, I crossed the room to the bookshelf that Lucas had put in for me. I hadn't put many books on it yet.

Picking one, I plopped onto the couch and stared out the window at the snow that had begun falling an hour before. I was determined. This was going to be a good Christmas for everyone, despite everything that I had caused. Natasha and Lucas, because it was our first holiday season as a family. Monica and her girls, because I'd taken so much from them unintentionally.

I curled up on the couch, looking at the clock. It was eleven a.m. and I had two hours before Lucas would be home from his shift with the soup he'd be picking up. Sounded like it was time for a cozy reading session.

CHAPTER TWO

LUCAS

"I'll see you tomorrow, Nick!"

My eyes swung across the police station and landed on the empty desk across from mine. I jerked inadvertently. My brain still expected to see my redheaded best friend, and partner, sitting there waiting to bounce ideas off of or asking where we could go get lunch. Looking over at Nick finally, he smiled understandingly and nodded his head.

"See you tomorrow, man," he replied.

I hated that. The fucking look of pity from everyone. We were a close department and everyone liked each other, but everyone knew Paul and I had been best friends for nearly my whole career. He'd gotten a job and moved here right when I'd started. I'd grown up in the community and had been thrilled to become an officer here myself. He'd met my friend Monica and fallen in love. They'd gotten married and he'd become a father to her oldest and they'd had their own daughter. I had never imagined a day where we would have to live without him. Yet, here we were.

It was a catch twenty-two. If he hadn't been brave and went in after Becks without back-up, I wouldn't have the love of my life, and my daughter, today. I just wished I hadn't had to lose my best friend to get everything I'd wanted in life.

Shaking my head, I walked out of the precinct and down the street to the local cafe that Becks and Monica frequented. I glared up at the gray sky that was spitting snow down on me.

Rebecca loved this shit while I preferred sunshine. I didn't care what the temperature was if the sun was out. Rebecca preferred cloudy weather with some kind of precipitation. The fact that it was cold, cloudly, *and* snowing was a travesty. Knowing Becks, she was at home giddy over the weather.

Stepping into the cozy cafe, the bell hanging above the door rang and I grinned at the woman behind the counter.

"Hey, Lucas," she chirped, tossing her blonde pony-tail over her shoulder.

Caroline Foster was back in town. She'd graduated college with a degree in marketing and worked for some large company in the city for years. Suddenly she was back home without explanation. Her parents owned this restaurant and she'd immediately claimed she'd rather work for them than some corporation anyway. There was a story there, her eyes had changed. Some of the light had gone out in them. With this town, everyone was already speculating and the rumor mill was in overdrive.

"Caroline," I greeted. "How're the folks?"

"Good. How're Becks and Nat?" she smiled up at me, her blue eyes sparkling.

"They're good. Becks called me earlier and Nat has the bug

that's been going around the schools. I was wondering if I could get a few quarts of your chicken noodle soup?"

Her sympathetic eyes met mine.

"Of course. Oh no. That sweet thing. I hope she gets better in time for the school Christmas parties."

I smiled in acknowledgement and watched her get to work, ladling soup into containers as I checked my phone.

"It's on the house for our favorite police officer. I also added half a dozen chocolate cupcakes for when Nat feels better." I looked up as she pushed the two brown bags across the counter.

"Caroline, you didn't have to do that. I can pay."

She waved her hand in my face, laughing.

"I know you could pay, Lucas. You know Mom and Dad like to give back to the community. You protect this community. Don't worry about it. Just get home safely and take care of your girls."

"Well, thank you. Have a good day." I returned, nodding my head. Turning I glared out the window, cursing Mother Nature, before stepping into the snow that was coming down heavier than before.

Opening the door to the comfortable home I'd inherited from my Nan, I kicked off my boots. I made sure to shake the snow off of everything and hang my coat in the closet before completely entering the house. I knew Becks was adjusting to living with someone and my habits tended to annoy her at times. I was trying my best to adjust how I did things. It was quite the learning curve, living with someone for the first time in ages. I could smell cleaning products and glanced around. A blanket and book lay on the couch, forgotten. This woman couldn't relax for longer than fifteen minutes. It had been worse recently.

"Becks!" I yelled, softly, not wanting to wake Nat up.

"Kitchen!" I heard my fiancée's raspy voice reply.

Picking up the bags of soup and cupcakes I smiled and hurried through the warm living room to get to her. No matter how many days I came home to this woman, I couldn't help the feeling of excitement I got before I set eyes on her. I couldn't believe she was mine.

My fiancée was in the kitchen of my home, waiting on me after work.

"What in the hell are you doing, Rebecca?"

All jovial emotions faded out as I stared, mouth hanging open at my curvy fiancee, on her tiptoes, on the kitchen counter, stretching towards the top of the cabinets.

"Cleaning." She smiled at me over her shoulder, continuing on with her business like nothing was the matter, and my heart wasn't beating out of my chest. I knew women were strong and capable creatures, but she could fall and break her neck and she was here without anyone to catch her if she fell.

"You couldn't wait until I got home to at least spot you? Didn't you just clean those last week?" I grumbled, setting the bags of food on the bar and moving to stand behind her. I stared at the back of her legging-covered knees.

Damn. Even the back of her legs turned me on.

"I didn't wanna bother you when you got home. I had the time," she shrugged one shoulder, not even turning to look at me.

I quirked an eyebrow and began to lift my eyes up towards her head, but stopped at her ass, shamelessly checking her out.

"Could've fallen and broken your neck." I said, distracted now.

"It's fine, grouch. I'm almost done. What do you think I did all those years without you?"

I scowled up at her cheeky face looking down at me. I hated when she brought that up. I knew she'd been alone, handled herself and a child for years. I knew she'd done everything independently, but she didn't have to now. I was here. I was supposed to help shoulder her burdens.

"Alright, sassy," I reached up with my big hands, tattoos covering the back of them, and gripped her waist from behind. Running my palms up under her shirt, meeting bare skin.

Becks scowled down at me as she bent her legs, lowering to move down.

"Now who's going to make me fall?" she asked, breathlessly, but she couldn't hide the heat in her eyes. I helped her down, spinning us to press her into the counter.

"I missed you," I murmured against her lips before kissing her deep. I stroked the seam of her lips gently and she parted for me like she always did. Our tongues dancing together as her hands moved up my back, scorching through my uniform shirt.

"You just saw me eight hours ago," she gasped, breathlessly. Her chocolate eyes gazed up at me in a daze, and I smirked.

"Nat still asleep?" I asked softly, bringing my hand up to brush her hair off her forehead, tucking it behind her ear.

She nodded, "Sleeping is the best thing for this bug, it seems."

"Good."

I swept down, kissing her harder and deeper as she groaned. Wrapping her arms around my neck, she raked her fingers over the back of my scalp and through my hair as I ground my hips against her. All I had to do was sense her being near me, catch a whiff of her shampoo or some shit, and I got hard. My hands wandered down her sides, under her shirt, then back up over her stomach and covered her breasts, kneading them through her bra. I loved how soft she felt, warm and cozy, even as she shivered from my hands being outside in the cold.

I felt her nipples pebbling beneath the fabric of her bra and focused on them, circling them with my thumbs while we kissed each other senselessly. She was always so responsive when I touched her here. There were a few times I was sure she was going to come just from the stimulation to her nipples. It turned me on to no end and I was determined someday she would.

"Lucas," she moaned softly, pulling back, panting softly.

I simply kissed down her neck, sucking and biting as I went.

"I need you, woman," I growled.

Suddenly, I had to have her. It was always like this with us.

"Yes," she pleaded, pulling me closer to hold me tight against her.

I looked down into her eyes again.

"Turn around, baby."

I guided her as I spoke, running my hand over her spine to bend her over the counter, gently.

"Stay."

I smiled as she whined softly. She hated being told what to do outside the bedroom, but when my hands were on her, she liked to listen. Slipping my hands into her leggings, I drew them and her panties down to her ankles.

Drawing up to my six-foot-six height, I growled looking down at her bare and wet for me.

"Spread your legs for me, Becks," I ordered softly, watching her. She wiggled her hips and adjusted her stance until it was wider. Opening herself to me, so beautiful and trusting.

I unbuckled my belt and undid my pants quickly. Drawing myself out through my boxers, I gripped the base of my hard length and rubbed the tip of my cock through her wetness teasingly, bracing myself over her, groaning.

"Jesus, baby. You're so wet for me." I said as she moaned and moved her hips back against me. She liked it when I talked dirty to her.

"Lucas, please," she begged softly.

I looked down at her, laying bent over our kitchen counter, spread wide open and dripping wet.

"Use your words, sweetheart," I teased, barely pressing inside her.

"Please, fuck me," she whispered, glancing over her shoulder at me sassily.

I groaned.

Usually it took some coaxing and teasing to get her to break, but my girl must've been needy for me. Pushing in a few inches, I pulled out again as she moaned, her palms sliding against the counter. Pushing in further this time, I continued the process giving her time to adjust to my length. She always needed a minute. She was so damn tight.

"You with me, sweetheart?" I rasped, stroking up her spine with one of my hands, the other braced on the counter beside her, finally seating myself all the way inside her, my hips pressed against her ass, her pussy taking me in deep.

"Yes, please, fuck me, Lucas."

That's all I needed to hear. My hips started snapping back and forth, driving her into the counter as her hands grasped against the wooden countertop, trying to find purchase. The wet sounds of my cock entering and exiting her echoed through the kitchen, flesh meeting flesh. Her pussy spasmed around me as I moaned. Her breath hitched as I hit that perfect spot inside her.

I looked down at where I entered her, taking in how she accepted me into her body, her thighs already trembling.

"Are you gonna come for me, Becks?" I asked, voice sounding like I had swallowed rocks.

"Yes, please," she moaned.

"Shhhhh," I soothed, leaning down, moving my hand until it wrapped around her neck, drawing her back up against my chest, squeezing gently.

"Gotta be quiet, Becks" I whispered, my breath hot and wet against her ear. "Gonna come all over your cock?" My other hand drifted down, finding her clit and rubbing it in small gentle circles as she nodded frantically.

"Lucas," she exhaled louder, as my hips pounded into her faster, deeper.

My hand moved up from her throat, covering her mouth.

"Come for me, Rebecca" I ordered, "Fuck. Come with me, baby."

I felt her tremble against me, her pussy squeezing my cock tight inside her as she orgasmed. Her cries were muffled against my hand as she clutched at my arm with both of hers holding on for something to ground her.

Groaning, I slammed my hips against her one last time, driving deep, and emptying myself inside her, panting.

"I love you so fucking much, Rebecca." I whispered, moving my hand off her mouth back to her throat.

"I love you too." she whispered, sighing contentedly. She laid her head back against my shoulder and smiled up at me. Her cheeks were pink, face flushed with her orgasm, but I knew she still felt shy sometimes.

Withdrawing from her and turning her gently, I pulled her panties and leggings back up, smiling with satisfaction that I'd be dripping out of her the rest of the day.

"You caveman," she teased.

"Only for you." I replied, tucking my cock back into my boxers and pants and rebuckling everything. "Does something to me to know I'm all over you and you're all over me." I kissed her gently.

She smiled up at me, rolling her eyes, as she stepped away to open the bags.

"Cupcakes too?" she asked, shaking her head, thinking I'd spoiled Nat.

"Caroline sent them. Said she hoped she felt better soon. She let us have it all on the house."

I watched Becks' face as she gasped, staring at me.

"She didn't have to do that!" she exclaimed.

"I know, I told her that. They do that for the servants of the community sometimes. Get used to it, Becks. We're a community that takes care of one another."

She shook her head, staring at the three quarts of soup and half a dozen chocolate cupcakes.

"I don't know if I will ever get used to it," she admitted softly.

I nodded knowingly. My fiancée struggled to accept help

and did so sparingly. Sometimes I had to pry it out of her. I leaned over, kissing her forehead gently.

"I'm gonna go check on Peanut," I said.

She nodded, already distracted and moving away to pour the soup into a pot to heat, and plating the cupcakes.

I smiled, turning and leaving the kitchen.

CHAPTER THREE

BECKS

"Can you grab the salad while I get the cake?" I looked over at Lucas as he pulled into Monica's freshly-plowed driveway a couple of days later. I'd bet money that Trevor had been here to do this for her. Lucas nodded, squeezing my thigh, and smiling over at me.

Nat was already squealing and leaping out of the back of his huge, black truck. She had gone through roughly thirty-six hours of fevers and body aches. She'd only been sick twice more and had been happy to get back to school to close out the semester before Christmas break.

"She's gonna break her freaking neck." Lucas griped, rushing after her. I laughed, shaking my head at both of them.

We usually met at Monica's house, or her and the girls came to our house, for dinner once a week.

I jumped down from my side of the truck as Lucas started towards the house with the salad, yelling at Nat to slow down.

Opening the back door to my side I reached in to grab the cake I'd made that afternoon. Lucas was going to grill some chicken that Monica had marinating. He was in a hurry to get to the patio and a cold beer despite the winter weather.

I knew he still struggled coming over here and not having his best friend to share a beer and hold down the grill with. Nat and Lexi usually ended up out in the backyard with him instead, showing off their cartwheels or volleyball moves. With the snowfall I was positive there would be some kind mischief.

The girls were more intuitive to our feelings and emotions than we often gave them credit for and they could tell Lucas missed Paul and provided distractions for him. I grabbed the cake and shut the door as Lucas disappeared into the house.

Monica was standing in the doorway waiting on me as I walked around the back of the vehicle. I smiled and waved at her. I was watching my steps as the snow and ice on the ground were slippery when they froze over again in the evenings. I was a klutz without the hazardous conditions.

Just as I cleared the back corner of the truck to start up the sidewalk a shot rang out over the neighborhood and I didn't even think. The cake upended from my hands and landed, chocolate strewn across the pristine snow. My knees hit the ground, provided a slight cushion with the powder, as I covered my head with my arms. My heart felt like it was trying to crawl out of my throat as I gave a small scream.

My entire body was frozen and the blood was rushing in my ears as my brain rapidly fired information through my head. We were in a suburban neighborhood in Reading, Pennsylvania. Who would be shooting at us? Fight or flight be damned, I was frozen in fear.

I was in a memory six months earlier, fighting and screaming to get to Paul. He was shot in front of me and bleeding out. "Tell my girls I love them, Becks. Tell them for me."

I thought I was crying, I knew I was hyperventilating, but it was so cold I couldn't tell. I heard voices yelling faintly. The blood rushing in my ears wouldn't let me focus on much for long.

"Becks," a gentle voice said.

Monica's soft hands touching my arms and pulling me up gently. I met my best friend's eyes, reality crashing back in around me.

"It was a truck backfiring, hon."

She was speaking softly, like she was dealing with a frightened animal. Her eyes were crinkled behind her glasses in worry and she had to be freezing. She'd kneeled in front of me in the snow in her leggings and sweatshirt, barefoot and messy ponytail.

"Becks?" Lucas' gruff voice came from above us as he ran up. "Shit," he had his large hand under my arm and one under Monica's helping us up. Once he made sure Monica was steady, his gaze swung solely to me. His gray eyes taking me in. I was still trembling so hard I felt faint.

"Deep breaths with me, baby girl," he said, softly and coaching, like my therapist had shown him.

"What's going on?" Monica asked softly, behind him, "How long has this been happening?"

"We'll talk in the house," Lucas replied, guiding us both inside. Leaving the chocolate cake and its pan discarded in the snow, forgotten for the moment.

As he settled me on Monica's plush, comfy couch, she draped

a blanket over me. Lucas knelt in front of me, trying to meet my gaze, his large hands rubbing my thighs as my breaths calmed.

"Tell me what's wrong," Monica demanded, getting frustrated with us both.

"Becks has still been struggling with everything that happened," Lucas explained softly. His gray eyes still meeting mine, rubbing my arms, trying to warm and soothe me, "She's been seeing a therapist weekly to deal with the trauma from the relationship with Clark, running for so long, and the kidnapping. She's been doing better. This was out of the blue. Her anxiety has been worse lately."

"God," Monica whispered, sitting beside me and drawing me to her. I still felt numb, weak, and embarrassed. "Why didn't you tell me?" she asked tearfully.

I shook my head, at a loss for words or explanation. Here she sat taking care of me when it was her that had lost her husband in a tragedy.

"She didn't want to worry you. You're still grieving too," said Lucas, gruffer now, frustrated himself because he'd tried to get me to talk to her.

"I told her she should. She needs support and she knows she has it. Stubborn, independent woman."

I glared at him and took a deep, shaky breath.

"I don't know. Things have been worse this month again." My voice came out frailer than usual, unlike how I typically spoke. "My therapist actually…" I broke off, realizing I hadn't even shared this with Lucas yet because I hadn't wanted to worry him.

His eyes narrowed on me and so did my best friend's.

"Tell us," She demanded, crossing her arms in front of her.

"She said the therapy has helped. Talking it out, and it definitely has." I continued, their shapes blurring as my eyes filled with tears. I hated admitting weakness and defeat and this was the equivalent of that to me. It was like I was still giving Clark power over me.

What if it was too much for Lucas finally? The months of nightmares, flashbacks, and PTSD.

"Becks. I'd hope you know by now that nothing you can say would ever change my feelings for you. I'm all in. I'm here, baby. I'm never going anywhere. You've dealt with a lot of trauma. Abuse, running, being alone, then being kidnapped, and killing two people, even though it was in self defense. Sweetheart… You're allowed to need help." His large hand rested on my face, thumb brushing some tears that were falling

Monica was nodding frantically beside him and tears were rolling off her face too. Both of our tears, falling into our laps.

"She thinks I need medication. For the attacks, and to get better sleep. I haven't been sleeping…" I whispered, "Especially when you're on night shift."

Lucas' brows came together, "Becks…" he sighed, like I had broken his heart. "Why didn't you say anything?"

Mon was sniffling beside me.

"Would you stop being so freakishly strong?" She demanded, abruptly.

My eyes swung to hers. We were both sobbing messes.

"There's no shame in therapy. In medication. I've been taking something for anxiety for years. You need to take care of yourself and let us help you. You're not alone anymore. You're not alone, Becks."

"I just don't know what the breaking point is going to be!"

I blurted out. "When am I going to be too much? When will I have finally taken too much from all of you?"

Lucas' jaw tightened, clenching his teeth.

"Never." He promised. "That's what a real family, and real relationships look like, Rebecca. I know Monica feels the same way. That's not how this friend group operates. Never has, and never will, sweetheart."

Monica was nodding emphatically.

"Becks, none of us could ever expect you to get over everything immediately. No one can do that. If you did, we'd be worried. And I honestly kind of have been. You're always taking care of everyone else. Let us help. Paul wouldn't have wanted this. We knew Paul. Paul loved you because you loved his best friend and brother. And he loved you because you loved me."

I was crying again. A snotty mess as Monica and I fell into each other's arms in a hug.

"Alright then. I'm gonna let you two talk. I'll start the grill and check on the girls. But we're talking about this later, Rebecca." He stated this softly, but firmly.

I nodded, wiping the tears from my cheeks onto my shirt's sleeves.

He leaned down, kissing my forehead, his short beard scratching my skin. He felt like home and I didn't know how I'd ever survived without him. I breathed in his scent before he stepped away, grounding myself.

As he left the room, Monica squeezed my hand, "Talk to me." She pleaded softly. "Really talk. Don't just tell me what you think is safe for me to hear."

"I just don't know, Mon," I answered "I truly didn't do this to hurt anyone. I've had it under control and things have been good again. It's just…I think my anxiety is off the charts because of learning to adjust my life. Living with Lucas. Having friends. Sharing Nat. Dealing with everything. I'm still processing. It's amazing Lucas talked me into seeing a therapist."

Monica sighed, pulling her legs up under her to sit back against the couch gazing at me.

"And the therapy is helping?"

I nodded, picking at the blanket anxiously.

"It is. It's just been bad lately. I've been worried about Lucas. He's been taking a lot of night shifts lately. And… he's been on the phone a lot. He won't tell me who he's talking to. I know he'd never…"

Monica's eyebrows drew in. "He wouldn't cheat on you, Becks. Lucas adores you and that little girl. He has been the happiest I've ever seen him outside of having lost Paul."

I nodded in acknowledgment of that, staring at my fingers pulling on the loose threads.

"I know," I said. "It's just weird. He's usually so open and not so secretive. He hated the night shift and being away from us…" I trailed off shrugging, "I can't sleep when he's gone. I feel like such a baby. I lived alone for years and now I'm this reliant mess."

"Maybe they've needed him to pick up some slack. Night shift pays more and it is his first Christmas with a significant other and kiddo." She pushed my arm gently.

I tilted my head. "We told each other no grand gestures. I don't need anything." I argued.

Monica snorted a laugh and raised her eyebrows.

"Whatever. That man has something planned I bet. Stop worrying. Communicate. Try the sleep medication at least,

Becks. We want you to be okay. Maybe Lucas could put an alarm system in if he's going to continue working nights regularly."

I sighed and nodded.

Shrieking from outside made us both look over towards the kitchen as Nat and Lexi ran in covered in snow and dripping wet.

"Uncle Lucas cheats!" Shrieked Monica's youngest shaking her red hair and sending drops of melted snow all over the kitchen counter.

Nat was giggling hysterically.

"Dad got us good!" She squealed, her blue eyes sparkling.

Every time I heard her refer to Lucas as Dad my heart grew a couple of sizes like the Grinch, I swear.

"You two, take your shoes off right there and get upstairs and dry off. Nat, surely Lexi has something you can wear or you've left something here at some point," laughed Monica. "You both just got over being sick! That man."

I laughed and my best friend's eyes met my own in relief at the sound.

"Do what Monica says, girls," I shook my head. "I wonder if Lucas looks just as bad?" I questioned. "Think he's even paying attention to the grill?"

Monica laughed and got up, walking into the hall to the linen closet. Grabbing two towels she walked over to start wiping the kitchen floor.

"I know you love this weather but I cannot wait for spring!" She exclaimed. "Everything is cold and wet and just yuck."

I stood to walk over to the stove.

"I'm gonna make some hot cocoa for everyone. I know it's before dinner but apparently we have some frozen popsicles for family members right now."

Screaming erupted from upstairs and Lacey, Monica's oldest, yelled at the two younger ones.

"THAT'S COLD!"

Monica grimaced at me and headed for the stairs, "I'm off to save our young ones from the monster!" She claimed, heading up the stairs.

I nodded, continuing to throw ingredients into the pot on the stove to make the cocoa. I took a deep breath and let the movements relax me further.

I had finally stopped shaking and the movement of something I'd done hundreds of times before was relaxing me. Grabbing some mugs from the cabinet, I smiled as I listened to Monica yelling at the three teenagers upstairs.

CHAPTER FOUR

LUCAS

I sighed, staring down at the chicken cooking over the hot coals. Some may think we were insane for grilling in the winter, but it was soothing.

I smirked as I heard the girls shrieking while Monica and Becks laughed. It was good to hear Becks laugh. She didn't do enough of it in my opinion. If I could take every painful thing from that woman, I would.

I couldn't believe she hadn't told me about how bad things were getting again. What the hell could have been bothering her so bad she was regressing with her reactions? I needed to do better and pay more attention. The fact that she wasn't sleeping because I was working night shifts made me feel like an ass. I wasn't really working extra shifts at night. I was sneaking off to work on a Christmas present for her. I couldn't have anticipated it affecting her like that. She'd lived alone for so long before me.

We'd promised each other no grand gestures, but fuck that. I knew my girl hadn't gotten anything for Christmas since she was in high school. That wasn't gonna slide with me. She deserved the world. She had given so much of herself to her daughter the last thirteen years, Becks needed to feel treasured too.

Nat was in on it, but I hadn't told Monica. She had enough on her plate. Mon knew I was planning something epic, but not details. Nat was so excited that she could help and give her mom something besides a school craft for Christmas.

I loved this. Parenthood was a learning curve, but it just felt right, being this little girl's dad. I could not wait to stand up and marry her mom and make everything official.

I just wished I could break down the last few barriers Becks had around her. Seeing her guarding her emotions and her fear of being left, were getting to me. I didn't know how much more I could show and prove that I wasn't going to disappear. Now that I knew she was struggling this badly again I needed to figure something out.

"Do you want some cocoa?" Becks' voice sounded like it usually did now. I smiled at her over my shoulder, letting my eyes run over her, checking in. She looked better and the light was back in her eyes.

"Sure, baby."

I watched as she stepped out with an oversized mug that was steaming, and met her halfway. She smiled up at me as she put the warm ceramic in my hands and I leaned down to kiss the tip of her nose.

"You know I love you more than myself, right?" I asked, my voice rougher than I intended. Her palm met my cheek and she smiled at me again.

"I know, Lucas. I'm sorry it's been such a mess with me lately-"

I shook my head, cutting her off, "Being with you, doing this life with you, has been anything but a mess. It's brought me a reason, Becks. I just want you to feel like you can talk to me. About anything. Always."

She nodded, crossing her arms, and I pushed her back towards the house gently.

"It's too cold out here without a coat. We'll talk later. Get your gorgeous ass inside. Tell Monica the chicken is almost done."

She laughed and walked back inside, quickly shutting the door behind her. I could hear her yelling for Mon and shook my head.

"You'd have some good advice for me, I'm sure," I muttered under my breath to Paul, wondering if he could hear me wherever he was.

My redheaded best friend had always helped me with stuff, and talked things through with me. I hadn't truly appreciated it until it was too late. I wondered if I'd ever stop talking out loud to him when I was alone.

I jumped as my phone rang, reaching into my pocket. *Nan.* I grinned, answering.

"Hey, Nan." I greeted.

"Lucas, how are you?"

"Good, how are you? Behaving yourself?"

Nan snorted, "What trouble could an old woman like me get into?"

I laughed outright at that.

"Too much to name. What's up?"

"I just wanted to check in on my grandson. See how my girls

are. I feel like I haven't seen you in ages."

"Nan, we were over for dinner last night."

We talked daily and ate with her once a week, but she'd gotten so attached to Nat and Becks that she was always sniffing about it being forever since we'd seen her.

"I know. I just love seeing them. Nat keeps me young."

I chuckled, "She is a special little person isn't she? We're all fine, Nana. What if we all come by tomorrow before I take Nat shopping for Becks?"

"Oh, are you still working on Becks' Christmas surprise?" She asked.

"I'd say I have about three more days on it. It'll be done by Christmas Eve."

"She's going to be beside herself," said my Nan, knowingly.

"I know."

"Well. I'll let you get back to it. Give the girls my love. Behave."

"I will. Love you."

"I love you too, Lucas."

Hanging up, I placed my phone back in my pocket and took the chicken off the grill. Walking back into the house I set my half-empty mug of cocoa on the counter beside the finished chicken.

Monica thanked me and I took my coat off, watching her and Becks move around the kitchen seamlessly. They were laughing at some scenario from one of the fantasy romance books they were reading together. I couldn't keep track of their stories and authors. Some fairy or monster romance stuff. Embarrassed the hell out of Becks when I'd read one but couldn't say she cared when I'd reenact a scene for her.

Lacey, Lexi, and Nat ran in, the younger two giggling and driving the elder crazy.

"Girls. Please stop pestering your older sister," Monica groaned while Becks set the sides and salad on the table.

"Like they'll listen," complained Lacey, scowling at the grinning younger girls.

I threw my arm around my oldest niece's shoulder, placing my cold hand on her and making her squeal.

"You're just as bad as the younger two" exclaimed Becks shaking her head.

"We can't let Lacey get too big for her britches." I said, winking at Nat and Lexi while Lacey tried to scowl at me.

"Let's sit and eat." Monica announced, as she carried Becks and her wine over to the table. "I think this is necessary." She quipped.

"Tell me about it," replied Becks.

Later that evening, back in our cozy home across town, I watched from the doorway of Nat's bedroom as her mother tucked her in. I walked across the room and grinned down at my daughter.

"You ready for a kickass Christmas break, Peanut?"

"Lucas!" exclaimed Becks as Nat giggled up at me. Her blue eyes were sparkling with mischief and she winked.

"What am I going to do with you two?" asked Becks, crossing her arms. "Don't get her all riled up. Night, Nat. Love you."

"Love you, Mom."

We watched Becks leave the room and I grinned down at Natasha again.

"Are you almost done with it?" she whispered.

"Almost," I whispered back theatrically.

She giggled again.

"I talked your mom into letting me take you for ice cream and shopping after seeing Nan tomorrow. We can finish up your part of the surprise then."

She nodded, "Alright. Thanks, Dad. I love you."

"I love you too, Peanut." I said, smiling.

Checking her window to make sure it was shut and locked, I watched her snuggle into her blankets.

No matter how many times this kid had called me Dad the past six months, I still couldn't get used to it. My heart melted a little more every time. She owned my entire heart, along with her mother. I wasn't sure I had actually been living before them. Clicking her light off and shutting her door, I headed back downstairs.

Coming up behind Becks on the sofa I kissed the top of her head gently before coming around and sitting down beside her. I took in my fiancee with her cozy Christmas pajama pants and had to laugh.

"What?" she asked, raising an eyebrow and setting her book aside.

"I'm pretty sure those are the exact pants you were wearing the day I met you."

Looking down, her brown eyes lit up. "I'm pretty sure you're right. What an impression."

"You made a hell of an impression." I said, resting my hand on her knee. So, what's going on, Becks?" I started softly.

Sighing, she drew her legs up beneath her and immediately avoided eye contact.

"Hey," I spoke softly and her eyes flicked up to mine, "Eyes on me when we have important conversations, sweetheart."

She nodded, "I don't know how to explain it, Lucas. Everything is great. Wonderful. It's just been such an adjustment learning to live with another adult these last six months. I guess my anxiety is amplified because of it. Plus I've not been sleeping because you've been working so much at night and…" she trailed off.

"I agree it's been a major adjustment for me too. But, Becks, if I'm doing something that's bothering you, you should be able to tell me. Even something little. I know you are dealing with more because of everything that happened. I wish I could take it all, baby. I wish I'd been able to get to you sooner."

Becks shook her head, leaning over and grabbing my hand.

"I know in my heart that it happened how it did for a reason, Lucas. I slayed my own monsters. I just hate that you lost your best friend in the process and my best friend lost her husband. Nat's best friends lost their father. It just still shocks me that none of you blame me. I keep waiting for the elephant in the room to make itself known. Someone to be bitter. Someone to just start screaming at me that it isn't fair."

Her voice broke, a tear slipping down her cheek in the lamplight.

"I'm just so used to the opposite of what everyone is giving me that I don't know how to accept it. I can't sleep and I'm tired. My anxiety is through the roof worrying about everything-"

"Becks, baby. No one is ever going to start screaming at you. It isn't fair, but we know it's not your fault. None of it is on you. Paul definitely wouldn't have wanted you to be having these thoughts. You can't help the actions of others. Clark and Larry are the ones that took him from us. And they almost took you too. You're not the only one affected by that night. When I close my eyes sometimes all I see is you losing consciousness. Not knowing if I'd ever look into your eyes again." Now I broke off, clearing my throat.

"I know we've all been affected." Her voice came softer, hesitant and unsure. "I just feel like you've been pulling away. You're working night shifts more and you've been taking weird phone calls off and on."

"Rebecca Wareman," I interrupted. "Do you think I'm stepping out on you?"

I watched her cheeks flush pink and her eyes dart down to our joined hands.

Fuck me. She did.

I sighed and tugged her closer to me.

"Did you ever stop to think that it's Christmas time? Santa's elves get up to all kinds of mischief."

"That's what Mon said but we promised each-"

"Becks. Stop. I wasn't gonna let our first Christmas go by without doing something for you. Plus, I have a little girl in on it, that's thrilled to give something, that's not, homemade to her mother for the first time."

"I cherish everything she's ever given me. Homemade or not," Becks whispered tearfully.

"I know you do. But you deserve what we've got planned. You're crazy if you think I've been cheating on you. You think I don't miss you these nights I've been working?" I asked.

"I just thought maybe you were getting bored or-"

"Does someone who's bored come home from work and bend their fiancée over the counter?" I asked.

She was fire-engine red now, avoiding all eye contact.

"There's never a damn minute that goes by that I don't want you. Every time feels like the first time, Becks. It gets better and better. Learning you and what makes you come apart for me?" I leaned over, pulling her into a hug, my hands trailed down her back, over her soft, worn band shirt. I couldn't feel the outline of a bra. She was completely ready for bed. I hardened in my own pajama pants.

Grabbing her hand tighter in mine, I brought it to the front of my pants, pressing her palm to where I was hard. She licked her lips and glanced up at me.

"That right there? You're the only one that can do that for me anymore, Becks." I said, voice low. "You're the only one I wanna lose myself in over and over again. Always."

My head came down, lips brushing against hers, "You're all I ever want or need anymore." Then I was kissing her, devouring her and licking into her mouth as she opened for me. Bringing my hand up I circled her neck and squeezed gently as she moaned softly against my mouth. I didn't know how many more times she needed to hear it or for me to show her she was all I ever wanted. But I'd spend all night trying.

CHAPTER FIVE

BECKS

Okay. When Lucas Marshall kissed me like this I felt like an idiot for ever doubting or questioning anything about our relationship. His hand tightened around my throat gently, not cutting off air, just giving me a pressure I'd come to crave from him. I moaned softly against his mouth as my fingertips inched up and under the waistband of his pajama bottoms. His kisses grew hungrier as his beard scraped against my skin deliciously.

When my palm met his hardness without any barrier between us he groaned and pulled back arching his hips so his cock moved in my grip.

I chased him with my lips and kissed him harder. Every time was like a wildfire through my nervous system. This man caused the most decadent reactions out of my body.

I sat back and released him as he growled softly and moved to grab me again but I laid my palm on his chest and shook my head. Crossing my arms over my front I grabbed the hem of my old shirt and drew it up over my head, baring myself.

"Fuck," he groaned. I watched his eyes dart to the stairs. "We need to go to our room," he emphasized. "What I wanna do to you isn't fit for anyone to walk in on. Let alone our little girl."

My core clenched and I giggled and then yelped softly as he scooped me up over his shoulder, grabbing my shirt as he went.

"Hush," he growled, continuing down the hall, into our bedroom and kicking the door shut behind him.

Slapping him on the ass I spoke, "Let me down. I was trying to seduce you."

Lowering me to my feet in front of him, I looked up into his gray eyes as he towered over me.

"Seduce me? Woman, I'm yours."

I snorted, giggling at him before dropping to my knees.

His gaze heated as my fingers found his waistband, tugging his pajamas down to his ankles. As his hardened cock came into my view, I leaned forward licking the tiny bead of pre-cum that was leaking from the tip.

"Becks," he groaned again, threading his fingers through my hair.

I'd never enjoyed doing this before him. He gave me so much power in the bedroom I'd come to enjoy sex in a way I'd never dreamed was possible. Sucking him into my mouth I swirled my tongue around him as my hand gripped his base.

"Fuck, baby. You're doing that so well."

I squirmed at his praise, my thighs rubbing together, wetness pooling at my core. Sucking harder I took more of him inside my mouth, looking up and meeting his heated stare as I did so.

"You own me, Rebecca." He growled into the darkened room. "You're it for me. You're my forever. Never doubt that." He thrust his hips gently as I took him to the back of my throat and he moaned again. His salty taste invading my senses. Then he was pulling me up by my arms and pushing me back onto the bed gently. Grabbing my pajama bottoms I lifted my hips and pulled them off, baring myself to him.

"God. You're not wearing underwear?" he rasped, "If I'd known bedtime would've been sooner."

I laughed as he grabbed my legs and spread them wide, allowing himself an unobstructed view of my center. I knew I was blushing. I never got used to this.

"Always so fucking wet and ready for me," he murmured.

"Rub yourself." He ordered.

Biting my lower lip, I ran my hand down my stomach and to the apex of my thighs. Gripping the sheet with my other hand as my fingers found my clit, I moaned as they brushed across it gently.

"That's a good girl," he said, eyes glued to what I was doing, "Keep going, baby."

Using two fingers I formed tight figure-eights across my clit, feeling more wetness pooling at my center, moaning as I arched my hips.

"Tell me what you want, Becks," he said, licking his lips.

"I want you inside me. Right now. I need you, Lucas." I panted.

Dropping my legs, he hit his knees, leaning down and licking up my center. I cried out and dug my fingers through his hair. He pushed his tongue deep inside me, wrapping a large arm around my left thigh and across my lower stomach. His thumb found my clit and stroked it in soft circles as I moved my hips against his face.

"That's it, Becks, ride my face," he growled against my core.

I shivered at the sensation of his lips brushing, and his voice vibrating, against me. He covered my clit with his mouth and sucked hard causing me to arch up off the bed.

"Lucas, please, I need you!" I sobbed.

He grinned up at me from between my legs and crawled up the bed beside me and laid on his back. Grabbing my arm he pulled me up and over him, until I was straddling him. My hands landed on his chest and I looked down into his gray eyes. He knew I still got flustered doing this. Being on top as a plus-size woman, made me self-conscious.

"Get out of your fucking head, Becks." He spoke, his left hand coming back to my throat. "I'm a big boy. Ride me. Take what's yours. I'm yours and only yours. I can take it."

I closed my eyes, moaning softly at his words. He always knew what I needed to hear. Lifting up I reached down with my right hand, gripping the base of his cock. Bringing it to my entrance, I teased the tip of him running it through my wetness.

His left hand tightened around my throat with his right gripping my hip.

Arching his hips he slipped inside me as I gasped softly, "Lucas."

"Take me, Rebecca. Fuck. Sit on my cock, baby."

Lowering my hips over him, I took him inch by inch as we both groaned at the feeling. There was always a fulfilling stretch when he moved into me and I relished it.

Moving up and down his length until we met and he was seated inside me fully, I clenched my hands on his chest, scraping my fingernails over him as I swiveled my hips.

I was panting and already breathless at the feel of him own-ing me. He said I was taking him, but he took me for his, no matter what position we were in.

He gazed up at me with his eyes darkened, running his large hands over my hips and up to my breasts squeezing them. I tilted my head back on a moan looking up at the stars through the skylight over the bed that allowed the moon and stars to illumi-nate us.

"You're so fucking beautiful," he whispered.

Looking back down at him I raised my hips and lowered them, starting a rhythm as his fingers found my hardened nip-ples, pinching and toying with them.

"Lucas," I gasped, squeezing him tight inside me.

He bucked his hips up, meeting me and driving himself deeper.

I cried out, "Oh God!"

I leaned forward to get a different angle and my clit brushed against the base of him sliding in and out of me.

"That's it, baby. God, you're taking me so fucking well. Are you already close, for me?"

"You feel so good," I moaned, moving my hips faster. I don't know how he made me and my body come to life like this so quickly. I was already on the edge of climax, our skin slapping against each other echoing through the room. "Please…"

He met me thrust for thrust, his right hand sliding down to my clit, rubbing it firmly with his thumb. My thighs started shaking as I dug my nails into his chest harder and he groaned in pleasure.

He looked down, watching where our bodies connected,

"Come for me, Becks. Take this cock and come all over it for me."

His words washed over me, heating my body further as I tensed and cried out. My orgasm hit me, stealing the breath from my lungs as I ground my hips against him, his thumb strumming my clit faster to draw out my pleasure.

Collapsing onto his chest he ran his hands down my back. I felt him shift under me, spreading his legs and bracing his feet on the bed below us.

"Lucas-"

"Hang on tight," he interrupted, banding one of his arms low on my back, the other one high up to hold me against him, his thighs spreading me wide with his feet braced against the bed. And then, he started pounding up into me.

I cried out at the sensation, unable to move with how he was holding me, only able to feel, clenching the sheet on either side of him.

"Lucas!" I yelled softly, as he moved faster, driving up into me harder. The wet noises echoing through the room were overwhelming my senses and making my body burn hotter as he fucked me harder, destroying me in the best possible way.

"Oh my…Lucas…it's too-"

"You're going to come again. You're going to come hard on my dick and soak it," he demanded.

My pussy clenched at his words and I couldn't catch my breath. Stars seemed to be bursting in my vision as I held onto the sheet, my cries were getting louder and I couldn't help it. I felt my second orgasm barreling in on me.

"Come. Now." Lucas practically growled, his whole body straining under mine, moving like a machine, his jaw clenched as he held himself back.

"I love you!" I cried out breathlessly as my second orgasm washed over my body causing me to tremble as waves of pleasure overtook me. My vision went white as I felt Lucas thrust once, twice more, and empty inside of me, moaning my name.

I laid on his chest, with him still deep inside of me, trembling in the aftermath, as his hands rubbed all over my back soothingly, both of us catching our breath.

"I love you more," he whispered.

CHAPTER SIX

LUCAS

"Do you think Nana made any cookies?" Nat's sweet voice came from the passenger side of my truck. I glanced over and met her sparkling blue eyes. I couldn't not grin back at her, even if I tried.

"Kid, now that you're in her life, she's making enough cookies to feed all the kids in town," I assured her, "If she doesn't have cookies made for you I'll fall right over. She makes cookies more often for you than she does me anymore." I pretended to be offended.

She laughed at me softly, looking out the window and shaking her head. I loved bringing her here. My Nan had adopted Becks and her daughter like they were her own. Becks had fallen in love with her feisty ways and Natasha was always a giggling mess at my Nan's shenanigans.

Natasha soaked up every bit of grandmotherly affection she could get and oftentimes seemed like she was making up for the childhood where she'd grown up missing these things. I would see Becks watching them together with tears in her eyes and I knew she regretted Nat never having this before. Not like they could help it with the cards they'd been dealt.

I knew Becks and Nat were looking forward to Nan's Christmas dinner this year. She always made a whole spread with turkey, ham, and all the trimmings. Becks hadn't had a meal like that since she was in high school and Nat had never had a huge family meal. It was going to be a huge year of firsts. Monica and the girls were coming too so they weren't alone on Christmas night. Paul and her two families had always done things on Christmas Eve.

I threw the car into park as Nat unbuckled, hopping out of the truck, and taking off running for the door as I followed more slowly. Becks hadn't been able to come with us tonight, having picked up some extra hours suddenly. She was going out for coffee and dessert with Monica afterwards.

We had done some more talking last night before falling asleep and while I'd set her mind at ease in some aspects I knew she was still filled with self-doubt. She'd been through a lifetime of having to question whether or not she was worth anyone's love. It was going to take a bit for her to feel like she was.

Natasha had no such problem.

She was throwing herself into whatever relationship she could. It terrified the shit out of Becks. The little girl suddenly had a grandparent, a father, aunt and uncle figures, and a sisterhood and friendship to thrive in.

Walking into the home, I caught up with Nat at Nan's door, knocking excitedly.

"Well, if it isn't my favorite great-granddaughter!" exclaimed

Nan, opening the door to greet the exuberant teenager.

"I'm your only great-granddaughter," laughed Nat, wrapping her arms around my Nan in a huge hug.

I watched her return the hug, running her hand over the back of Nat's head gently, holding on as long as Nat would let her and not letting go until she was ready. My heart grew every time I witnessed something like this. Everything settled within me, telling me this was right.

"Where's our Becks?" Nan's voice drew me back as she held the door wide for me to follow Nat in.

"She had to stay late at work tonight. Everyone's needing something extra clean and organized for the holidays."

She nodded understandingly as she shuffled over to her chair and sat.

"How's the surprise?" she asked, eyes twinkling.

"Mom is going to flip out!" Nat shrieked, "Everything looks amazing. It's almost done and she doesn't have any idea."

Nan caught my eye and raised a single eyebrow with a knowing grin.

"That sounds amazing, sweetheart. You're a wonderful daughter. Honey, why don't you run to the kitchen and get some of the cookies I just made for you?"

"YES!" she exclaimed, sprinting from the room.

"How is everything really?"

I sighed, sitting on the couch, and stared at my Nan, the woman who'd raised me and loved me. She was more of a mother to me than anything.

"Becks thinks I'm cheating on her or something." I blurted out, throwing my hands up into the air.

"What?" she stuttered, gaping at me.

"Ugh. Maybe not that extreme anymore. She had a moment of doubt. She's been dealing with extra stress, just learning to live with another person and be in a normal, functioning relationship. Her anxiety is at an all time high and with me telling her I'm working extra shifts at night, she's convinced herself I've decided she's not worth it."

"Oh, my poor girl," Nan shook her head, her hand covering her mouth. "Is she still seeing that nice therapist?"

"Yes." I nodded, running a hand over my trimmed beard. "Becks and I had a good talk yesterday actually. She even admitted she knows I'd never do that. It's just everything messing with her. It's all an adjustment. She hasn't had anything good in so long. I'm considering showing her the gift on Christmas Eve, instead of waiting. Nan, I worry I'm fucking everything up," I sighed.

"Showing her the gift early may be best. The poor dear. I cannot imagine everything flying through her head. Living with that kind of stress for so long and then having to teach yourself to be calm. There's nowhere for all that adrenaline to go anymore. You're not fucking anything up, young man."

I gaped at my Nan's language.

"What? You can say it and I can't?" she cackled.

"Jesus," I muttered.

Then something she'd said came to me. Somewhere for adrenaline to go.

"Uh-oh. You've got that look in your eye," chuckled Nan.

"Maybe she needs to take a class," I questioned out loud, "Self-defense, gun safety, kick-boxing or something. Everytime she hears something that sounds like a gun going off she's a nervous wreck."

"Or maybe she needs her man to teach her gun safety," said Nan softly, looking at me. "Having never fired one before and then having to do so twice? She took a life both times too-" her voice trailed off, "That's quite a lot, Lucas. Just give her time. You two will work things out."

"I know. It's just frustrating that I can't take it all away." I ran my fingers through my hair, letting my head fall onto the back of the couch.

"Patience. You're a good man. I know, I raised you." she proclaimed, winking and rising slowly. "I'm going to make sure Nat isn't eating the entire batch of cookies."

I nodded, glancing over to watch her shuffle out of the room. Taking a deep breath I just let myself rest within the moment. Hearing my Nan's familiar voice mixing with Nat's cheerful one. Being around all of my Nan's things and even the smell that was just her. It was home and comforting. She was the mother figure in my life. Everything was going to be okay. I knew that. I think Becks was realizing that. We had such a support system we couldn't help but make it.

Nat came back into the room holding a plate of cookies while Nan followed with some cold sodas and a deck of cards.

"Nan Vi said we could play rummy again!" Nat announced with excitement, plopping down beside me. "She beat you good last time, Dad."

I grinned and glanced over at my Nan, seeing her eyes water at what Nat had called me. She smiled at me warmly and shuffled the cards.

"Well I'll just have to kick both your butts this time, won't I, Peanut?" I challenged.

"We'll see about that," sniffed my grandmother.

"Can we get this one too?" Nat handed me another book. I glanced at the stack in the shopping cart and back at her expectant face. We already had boxes of books hidden at the house too.

"Fine," I conceded. I was too much of a push-over when it came to her. Becks was telling me so, regularly, but even I was starting to see it. "Three more and that's it though. I mean it this time."

We were in the local bookstore and I was letting Nat pick out her part of her mom's Christmas present. Books. So many new books. Becks had always bought them used and then donated them to the library when they had to run again. She'd never owned any because it would've been too much of a hassle to move them. She was in the habit now of trading them out when she was done even though I had a bookcase in the living room for her.

Old habits die hard.

Our surprise was going to change things though. She was going to be able to keep whatever book she wanted and loved. I would buy her signed copies. She could treasure them and read them again and again. I was going to spoil the hell out of her.

"Okay."

I watched Nat take off to find the rest of her present and grinned.

"Lucas?"

I jumped, turning around and seeing Monica standing there. "Oh! Hey, Mon."

"What are you and Nat doing?" she asked, definitely suspicious.

"Just letting Nat shop for Becks' Christmas present." I said, trying to appear nonchalant.

Monica leaned around me, taking in the books in the cart, her eyes nearly bugging out of her head.

"LUCAS!" she exclaimed. "Those will fill up that bookcase you bought her for the living room and then some."

"Oh…" I trailed off, "You think?"

"Yes. Jesus. What are you thinking, you goof?" she walked closer to the cart, looking at the titles we'd been picking out. "Are you nuts?" she laughed, looking up at me.

I sighed. I was busted. It was time to fill someone else in on my secret.

"Listen, Monica. If I tell you what's going on, you cannot breathe a word of it to Rebecca" I said.

Monia raised an eyebrow, "Now I'm even more intrigued," she grinned.

I leaned over, speaking softly to her, relaying everything that had been happening the last month, watching her eyes get huge, then start watering, until she was full-fledged crying in the bookstore. We were definitely drawing some attention to ourselves.

"Do you think she'll like it? Are these good tears?" I asked, unsure, patting her shoulder.

"Yes, you idiot. She's going to die when she sees what you've done for her, Lucas. Oh my God." said Monica, wiping her tears. "I'm going to go help Nat grab a few titles she may not know her mom likes."

"Oh yeah?" I asked, raising my own eyebrow now.

"You'll definitely like them too. Y'all can reenact scenes from them," she threw back her head, laughing as she walked away.

I laughed with her as she went off to search for Nat, feeling like a weight had rolled off my shoulders. If I told Becks' best friend what I was doing, surely she could help hold Becks off a few days.

"Don't think we need any help in that department!" I called after her, shaking my head. Maybe I could get Monica to help me with the decor part of the surprise. She knows what Becks likes.

CHAPTER SEVEN
BECKS

"And he says everything is okay, and he's just planning some epic surprise. But, my head is just not accepting that for whatever reason." I trailed off, looking across the cafe's table at my best friend. I ran my fingernail around the rim of the oversized coffee cup and sighed.

"Becks. Lucas Marshall is head over heels in love with you," Monica's voice was calm and soothing. She pushed her glasses up on her nose and tilted her head, "That man can't even imagine looking at another woman. I promise that whatever is going on, it's going to surprise you," she smiled, shaking her head.

"I know that look" I said, narrowing my eyes on her. "What do you know?"

"Nuh-uh!" she exclaimed. "I'm not saying a single word. I've sworn an oath to secrecy," she throws her hands in the air after pretending to lock her lips and throw away the key.

I heaved a dramatic sigh, scowling at her.

"Lucas wants to take me to the shooting range." I said softly, spinning the mug on the table.

Monica tilted her head, considering, sipping her own cappuccino.

"That may not be a bad idea, Becks. Your only experience with guns was traumatic and-"

"We don't have to talk about this," I blurted.

"Rebecca Wareman. My best friend went through something traumatic and life altering. You let me talk about Paul when I need to even though it brings back bad memories for you."

"That's different," I whispered.

"It's really not." Monica placed her hand over mine, squeezing gently. "It may be good for you to feel like you're in control of the situation with one. Learn how to handle it in a safe and controlled situation. Get used to the noise," she encouraged me. "Paul used to take me all the time." She shrugged, taking another sip of her drink.

"My instinct is just to stay the hell away from them," I said, eyes watering at the thought.

"I get that," my best friend replied, gently. "Maybe we can go together." She suggested. "Lucas could work with us both. Paul would hate for me to just stop."

I stared into my best friend's eyes, "You'd do that for me?"

"Becks. Any of us would do anything we could to help you," she stated firmly, shaking her head at me, "One day you're going to believe that."

"Are you and the girls still going to your parents, and Paul's parents, Christmas Eve?" I asked, changing the subject.

Mon nodded, smiling as the waitress set down our food. "It's going to be different but I don't think anyone's ready to stop tradition," she stated, taking a bite of her chocolate cake.

"Mmmmmmm," she closed her eyes. "Okay. This is amazing. Enough talking for now. More eating."

I laughed, taking my own bite, eyes widening at the rich flavor.

"See." Monica emphasized, pointing her fork at me, "Amazing."

"You're right. Less talking. More eating." I laughed.

After a few moments of companionable silence, she spoke up, so quiet i could have missed it.

"Trevor has been coming around a lot lately…" she trailed off, reorganizing her cake to the center of her plate.

My eyes shot up to hers, "And how do we feel about that?" I questioned, taking a sip of my Americano.

I watched my best friend shrug, seeming unsure and felt my heart ache a bit.

"I really think it may be out of obligation. Lacey and everything. The girls are understandably still reeling from losing Paul."

"I doubt it's an obligation, Mon. I've been around you two often enough to see he still has feelings for you."

She choked on the bite of cake she'd just placed in her mouth, and I slid her ice water over to her.

After she'd taken a sip she looked at me.

"Are you kidding me? It's only been about six months since Paul died. Trevor doesn't have feelings for me…it's been so long."

I shook my head, pushing my own empty plate away from me.

"You're not quite on the outside looking in. Don't sell yourself short, Mon. I understand it being super soon but you'll know when it's right. Paul wouldn't have wanted you to be alone forever," I said softly.

"I know. I just wish we'd had that conversation." She said, staring out the window. "I always brushed him off. It hurts to even talk about it."

I stared at her until she met my eyes again and smiled gently.

"Don't beat yourself up about it. I don't think I could handle having that conversation with Lucas either. At all."

"Well, do it," she encouraged. "It may hurt but it would be a lot easier than wondering 'what if'."

I nodded in understanding as the cafe owner's daughter came to our table with the check. I grabbed it before Monica could, speaking over her protests.

"It's on me," I spoke directly to Caroline, who grinned at me, "don't let her sway you."

"I would never," the sweet blonde said, taking my debit card and leaving to run it.

Monica's eyes trailed after her, "We should see if she wants to hang out with us sometime."

"That would be nice," I agreed. "She's probably feeling a little lost, being back in a small town after big city life. The rumor mill has kind of been brutal."

Caroline made her way back to us, sliding my card and the receipt to sign in front of me. "How are those sweet girls?" She asked us.

"Oh. They have you fooled." Laughed Monica. "They're all hyped up now that they're on Christmas break."

"Nat is the same. She's been with Lucas all day doing 'secret things' and is annoyingly excited about not telling me." I rolled my eyes.

"It wouldn't be Christmas without surprises," smiled Caroline. "Thank you all for coming in. Have a Merry Christmas!"

"You too, Caroline." I smiled softly at her.

There was definitely sadness in her eyes as she smiled back.

She had a beautiful smile, but it wasn't quite reaching her eyes.

"So, where did you run into Nat and Lucas?" I asked my friend as we gathered our things.

"Becks! You're horrible. I was sworn to secrecy. Stop it."

"It was worth a try," I grinned.

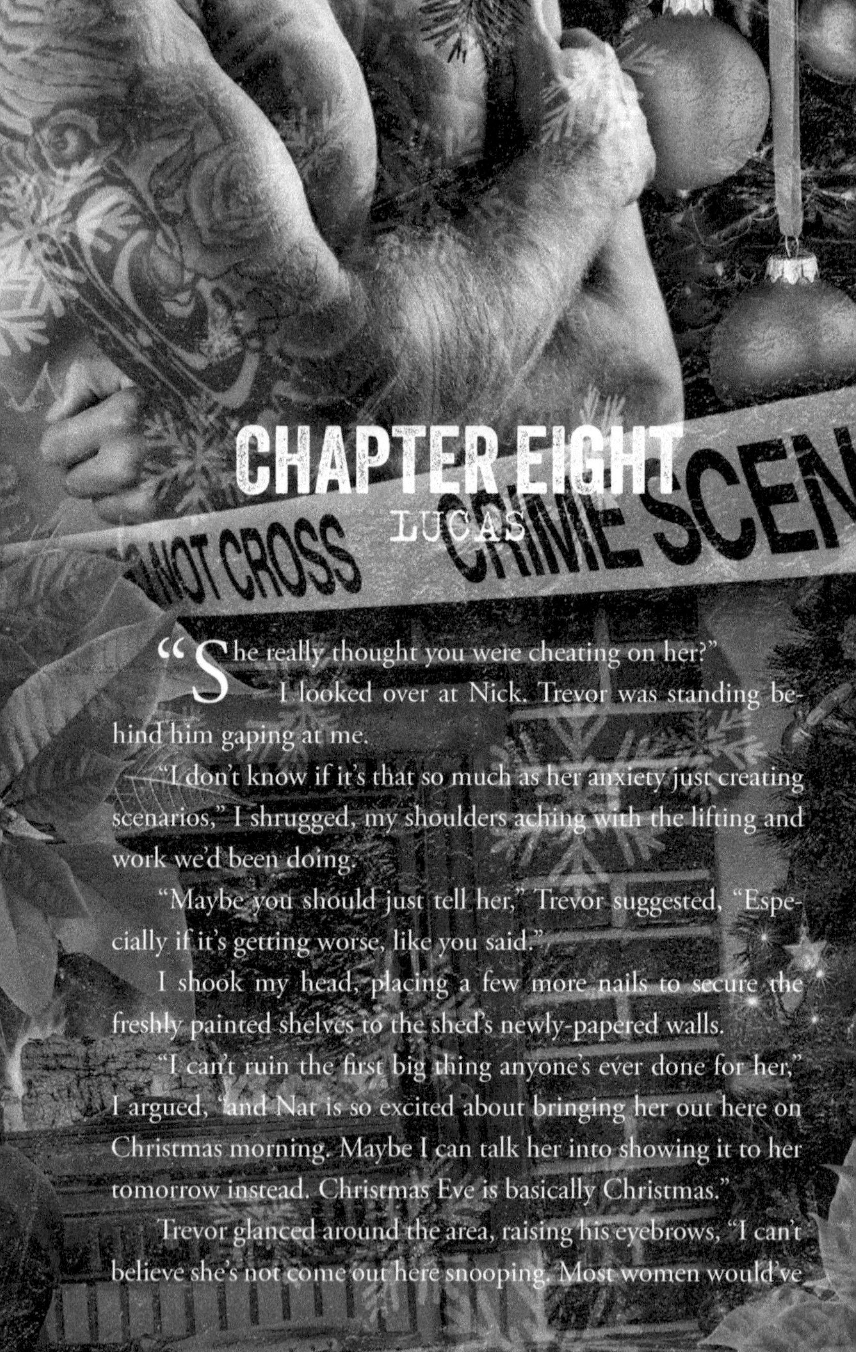

CHAPTER EIGHT
LUCAS

"She really thought you were cheating on her?"

I looked over at Nick. Trevor was standing behind him gaping at me.

"I don't know if it's that so much as her anxiety just creating scenarios," I shrugged, my shoulders aching with the lifting and work we'd been doing.

"Maybe you should just tell her," Trevor suggested, "Especially if it's getting worse, like you said."

I shook my head, placing a few more nails to secure the freshly painted shelves to the shed's newly-papered walls.

"I can't ruin the first big thing anyone's ever done for her," I argued, "and Nat is so excited about bringing her out here on Christmas morning. Maybe I can talk her into showing it to her tomorrow instead. Christmas Eve is basically Christmas."

Trevor glanced around the area, raising his eyebrows, "I can't believe she's not come out here snooping. Most women would've been digging around already. Is Mon still sneaking in tomorrow morning to place the books and decor before she heads to her parents?"

I laughed and nodded, "I told Becks there may be wildlife in this shed. It's so old that looking from the outside, there's no questioning it. It not having windows has helped too. I'm glad I ended up running into Monica and filling her in. I wouldn't know what books to put where."

"Driving you here from the station every 'night shift' you've been working has kind of been a pain in the ass," muttered Nick.

"I know. I owe you all. But man. She's gonna love this."

I stopped and looked around the space.

It had been my grandfather's woodworking shed. It was spacious and sat in the far corner of our back yard. The inside had been gutted and we'd lain new hardwood floors, wallpapered the walls, and hung soft lighting everywhere after redoing the ceiling. Fairy lights hung around the room with pictures of settings from her favorite books.

I'd added pictures of us and Nat, along with pictures of Monica and the girls. There was one of Paul and Monica with us on a date night too. The new sofa was big and comfortable. I'd even added one of those huge, comfy, lounge chairs she'd seen online, a small coffee bar loaded with all the ingredients and a few snacks, a mini fridge with other beverages and more snacks, and blankets. Lots and lots of blankets. The shelves wrapped around the entire room except for where furniture and the pictures were. There were also the boxes-upon-boxes of books and shelf decorations for Monica to place and organize.

The outside still looked like hell but that was getting redone this summer. Becks would have a library all to herself. I smiled taking in the work we'd done with pride.

"You're so gone," laughed Nick, shoving me.

"Hey. Don't hate what you don't understand," said Trevor. "If you love a woman enough, you'll do all this and more."

My eyes met his and I nodded at him.

I'd seen the way he'd been working his way back into Monica's everyday life. I'd always had the feeling he'd never let his feelings for her completely die. Paul had confided a lot to me about it and how he hoped if anything ever happened to him Trevor would find the courage to step back up. It ached to think about, but I couldn't say I disapproved.

Paul's understanding of the dangers of our job had made everything as easy as possible for Monica and the girls in the aftermath. It encouraged me to do the same and have my affairs in order should anything happen. I had Becks and Nat now, and as much as it pained me to think of leaving them in a world I wasn't in, it felt better knowing things were in order.

"Man," sighed Nick, oblivious to mine and Trevor's stare behind him as he finished placing another shelf. "I can't imagine being so gone over anyone to do all this. I've been alone so long I don't think I could cohabitate with anyone."

I shook my head at my friend. Nick was older than us by a few years and our group had always considered him the big brother figure.

"Those are the famous last words." I slapped him on the shoulder.

As we stood and surveyed the finished room, "I just want to say thank you all again for helping me when you could. I know you all have your own lives and are busy. I couldn't have gotten this done and together without you all."

"Our own lives?" laughed Trevor, "I'm basically alone and doing nothing when I'm not on shift or with Lacey," he scoffed, referring to his and Monica's daughter together.

"And I work and go home," added Nick. "This forced me out of my hermit tendencies."

"Think Mon will have enough time to get everything on the shelves and the boxes gone tomorrow?" asked Trevor, looking at the stack with some trepidation. "Are you sure you didn't go slightly overboard?"

"Nothing's overboard for Becks," I spoke softly. "Y'all know how Monica is. She'll have everything placed and put together within an hour. The best part is, Nat is going to spend the night with them tonight and she'll bring her over in the morning before she and the girls head out to her parents. The girls will be helping her."

Trevor nodded, "Gotta keep Becks distracted."

I grinned, "That won't be a problem."

Nick made a face. "Dude. TMI."

"Whatever, assholes. You guys are dismissed." I joked.

"Oh, okay, boss" joked Trevor while Nick mock saluted me.

I laughed as they walked out the door and disappeared into the night. Turning out all the lights, I locked up the door behind me and placed the key, and its new keychain, in my pocket.

I'd given Monica the second key earlier and everything was planned for her and the girls to park a street over and sneak in to finish the job. Walking in the back door, I overheard Becks telling Nat to be good as she was heading out the front to meet Monica and her girls for their sleepover.

"Hey! Don't forget to say goodbye to your dear old dad, Peanut!" I yelled.

I heard her feet running down the hallway as I exited the kitchen and scooped her up in my arms.

"Be good for Mon," I whispered, squeezing her tight, "Make sure everything looks perfect in the morning." I winked, setting her down.

She winked back, "I will. Promise. Love you, Dad."

"I love you too."

I watched her run past Becks at the front door and grab her bag on the way out.

Becks stood and waved as Monica honked and pulled away.

"So, what are our plans for tonight?" I asked, looking at my fiance.

She seemed on edge again today. I knew her anxiety was high again because of the first holiday without doom and gloom hanging over her head. She wasn't used to just being able to enjoy something without looking over her shoulder.

"Just wrapping the last of the Christmas presents," she murmured, moving past me and into the kitchen. "Can you grab them from the attic and bring them down? I already have the wrapping paper and stuff ready on the kitchen bar."

I nodded, turning and heading up the stairs. I pulled down the built-in ladder leading up to the attic and climbed a few rungs. I could grab a couple of bags from here with my height. I saw a wrapped package sitting by them that said my name from Becks. Shaking my head I knew she'd been climbing around the attic by herself again.

I sighed, pushing the ladder back up into the ceiling and turned. Nat's room looked like a tornado had hit it. I grimaced, knowing that irritated Becks. I also know she'd asked her to clean it before she left.

"That's not helping the anxiety," I muttered, flipping Nat's lights off and closing the door to her room. I picked up the bags of gifts and jogged down the stairs.

"Nat didn't clean her room?" I asked, walking into the kitchen. Becks stood with her hip against the kitchen bar looking at her phone. Loose curls fell around her face from her ponytail and she glanced up at me, eyes irritated behind her glasses.

"Doesn't look like it. I'm texting her now. I want it done before Christmas morning." she muttered.

"It looks like a typical teenagers room," I placed the bags on the bar, smiling at her.

Her phone hit the bar with a thunk and she straightened. "Typical teenager or not, I asked her to clean it before she went. I don't need everyone ganging up on me," she snapped.

My eyebrows raised. *Okay. Something else was going on here. Becks was never this short with me.*

"No one is ganging up on you, Becks."

She laughed and took out Monica and the girls' gifts. Reaching back into the bag she took out two manly looking presents and I knew she'd included Nick and Trevor.

My heart warmed a little bit. The second bag held several gifts for Nat, but as I watched her, I saw her hands were trembling. Leaning over, I moved the things she'd just taken out of the bags and placed my tattooed arms against the counter, looking up at her.

She scowled at me, but I could see something like pain lurking in her eyes. Maybe we'd finally reached a boiling point. I'd waited for this to happen. She'd never grieved or exploded after everything, might as well be tonight. Nat was out of the house and we could deal with this once and for all.

"What are you doing?" she asked with a huff, "I need to get these done."

"We have two days." I commented calmly, still looking at her. "Why don't you tell me what's bothering you, sweetheart."

"Ugh!" she slammed her palms on the counter "Not everything is a therapy session, Lucas."

I straightened, my own palms flat against the counter, "And how was therapy today?"

"Stupid."

My eyebrows raised further.

"Explain, Rebecca."

"I don't have to talk to everyone about everything!" she snapped at me.

"No. You see, that is the problem. You don't talk to anyone, about anything." I said, my voice louder now.

Instead of the fear coming across her face, that she usually got when I was frustrated and barely raised it, she squared up like she was going to go toe to toe with me. *Here we go. Finally.*

"You have no idea," she muttered, spreading some wrapping paper back out on the counter, moving to ignore me.

I swept my arm out, knocking it off the counter completely. She picked up the tape dispenser, tossing it at my chest. The small, plastic container hit me right in the middle of my casual tee and clattered to the floor. I glanced down at it and back up at her.

"Why don't you try using your words and telling me what the fuck is wrong, Becks?" I demanded softly.

Her hands went into the air and she honest-to-goodness stomped her foot.

"Everyone wants me to talk. Becks, you've been through

such trauma. Becks, you're too strong. Becks, tell me what's wrong-"

"Well to be honest, you're working yourself up into some kind of drill sergeant with cleanliness around here so everyone's walking around on egg shells for fear of pushing you over the edge. Why don't you go ahead and jump off it? Have at it! Do something, Rebecca. Explode. Rage. Break shit. Be pissed. Get fucking furious. Your therapist is right. You haven't grieved. You haven't even gotten mad. You're holding it all in and it's affecting your life and health. It's starting to affect our relationship and your friendships. I know it's related to your anxiety and issues here, but dammit. Nothing's going to get better unless you *Let. Me. In!*"

I watched her pacing back and forth from across the bar and slowly walked around to meet her coming towards me again. I grabbed her arms as I said, "Stop."

She yanked away, "Don't tell me what to do."

"Fucking talk to me."

She let out a frustrated little scream, placed her hands on my chest, and shoved. She caught me off guard enough I fell back a step, but grabbed her forearms again, and shook her gently.

"Let it out, Rebecca! Fuck! If you need to rage, rage at me. If you need to fall apart, I'll catch all the pieces and put you back together. If you need to hit something, hit me. I'm your safe place, Becks. Let it go."

CHAPTER NINE

BECKS

"*L*et it go."

Let it go? He didn't even understand what he was asking.

I didn't even completely understand what I was feeling.

I was suddenly just so tired of holding everything in and being strong. I felt like I was on the precipice of something and about to topple over into an abyss with no end in sight.

I immediately felt absolutely furious about everything that had happened to me.

Seeing everything good in my life, and watching Nat thrive infuriated me. We'd had that stolen from us for so long.

Seeing how everything should've been was breaking me.

Being scared of everyone leaving me was breaking me.

I was breaking myself.

I was projecting everything out onto everyone through cleaning and everything was manifesting through panic attacks and more cleaning.

I was infuriated that I'd been so stupid and needy that I'd been drawn to someone like Clark.

I was instantly furious that I'd been stupid enough to get in the car with Larry.

Me being stupid enough to get in that car was what led Paul away from his family, forever.

I saw my hand strike out and hit Lucas in the chest again.

He was braced this time and didn't even falter half a step. I wasn't strong enough to hurt him. I didn't want to hurt him. He was just there. Always pushing me to be better, and do better. I was mad at him for being so fucking perfect that I had to be scared every day that he'd disappear.

"That's all you got?" his voice grumbled down at me.

Suddenly my vision was clouded with moisture that wasn't because I was scared or anxious. They were furious tears that were coming from years of injustice and I kept slapping his chest with both hands, crying, and ranting about it all. Everything that I'd held in for over a decade was pouring out of my mouth.

My insecurities and fears rushed out from between my lips.

"Everyone thinks it's so easy," I gasped, not even recognizing my own voice through the angry sobs, "being so lonely without my parents and grandparents that I was stupid enough to fall for a monster like Clark. Ignoring all the signs and letting him brainwash me to believe I really couldn't do better. Letting him hit me and going back a second and third time. It took taking a fucking pregnancy test to wake me up, because I didn't value myself enough."

Lucas still just stood there. Silent and accepting of my palms slapping against his chest. Hearing the words I had never spoken aloud to anyone else. No matter how self-deprecating they were.

"Never letting anyone in. Never having friends. Having to fucking train my daughter to be secretive just to keep her safe. I ran and he still destroyed her childhood. I still feel like a failure of a mother because she just now gets to see what it should've been like. I hate myself every day I look into the mirror. I hate that I let it happen. I hate that she had to grow up that way. I hate that I ran and ran. I hate that he followed me. I hate that the first friend I've ever had lost her husband because of me. I hate that he felt like he needed to save me so he came in without waiting for help. I hate that I feel like I'm not good enough to deserve all of everyone's love and acceptance and understanding. I hate that I know deep down I do deserve it all and that none of it is my fault and the real problem is I just don't know how to fucking fix it!" I screamed the last part, shoving him and falling to my knees, even as he braced his arms around me and followed me down so I didn't hurt myself.

I covered my face as everything poured out of me, at long last. Having told someone my darkest thoughts and fears. Never having even voiced them to my therapist.

Lucas saw it all in the cozy kitchen of the house he grew up in.

He saw it all.

He'd let me use him as a punching bag and sounding board.

He'd dealt with me hanging on to the edge of a cliff for months.

He stayed.

He wrapped my daughter and I in so much love and understanding. I had been fighting this for months even though I knew I could talk to him. I knew he wouldn't go anywhere. No matter what I admitted or what I said, he would never leave me. Leave us.

I felt him sit on the floor beside me, leaned back against the bar. I felt his hand come around my arm and pull me gently until I was sitting across his lap. He pulled me against him, wrapping his arms around me, and holding me tight.

Lucas didn't share any words of wisdom.

He didn't start trying to pick up my shattered pieces laying open and bare.

Instead Lucas acted like the harbor in the midst of my storm, murmuring nonsense to me just so I'd know he was there when it was over.

My body relaxed against his bit by bit. My right ear was pressed against his chest, listening to the steady beat of his heart. Removing my glasses, I wiped my tears away on the sleeve of my sweatshirt, still sniffling. I was positive I looked disgusting. I could feel my ponytail hanging loose, pieces of hair stuck to my face with my tears. The front of my sweatshirt was soaked through from how hard I'd been sobbing.

"That was a long time coming," his voice rattled through his chest and I sniffed again even as I let out a pathetic laugh.

"I'm sorry," I whispered.

"Never apologize," he answered, running a large hand down my back. "You've been holding a lot of that in, for a lot longer than I even thought," he murmured, "But I do want to reply to a few things before we move on."

I sat still, snuggled against him, feeling like I'd been through a natural disaster. The adrenaline was leaving my system, leaving me weak and trembling.

"You, Rebecca Wareman, are anything but stupid." He

spoke softly, but firmly. "You were a young woman who had found herself alone in the world at too young of an age. Clark was a predator that was just waiting for that kind of person to cross his path."

I shivered and he tightened his arms around me.

"Clark got to you when you were lost in your grief. You were alone, scared, and hadn't ever gotten close to anyone. He was the first who'd shown you any affection or love in forever and he used it to his advantage. I hate that you didn't have someone who was enough of a friend to speak up and help. I hate that you were already such a closed off individual, because I think that made it even easier for him" he continued, "Whether you did or didn't leave? Whether you went back or not? Doesn't make you stupid. It was all you knew. It was all you'd had. He was the only constant in your life. No one is stupid for being scared that whatever is outside their nightmare may actually be worse. That positive pregnancy test? It woke you up. You were already a mother before you took it. You got over your fear of being alone and ran because you knew you needed to save your baby. That's the kind of badass woman you are."

I snorted softly.

"Don't do that. Don't sell yourself short. It took balls to run from that apartment that night. To pack a small bag and disappear. To face him in court and lie to save both your lives. That was badass. You are badass. That means you're also not stupid for getting in that car with Larry that day. You were saving your daughter's life all over again. You also didn't make Paul's decision for him. He chose to do what he did. He signed up for this life. He knew I'd have done the same if it had been Monica in that house. You're doing him a helluva disservice by not living your life to the fullest and counting his friends and family short. We don't have anything to forgive you for. You're not the monster that took him away from us. You didn't bring them here. That was their choice. Do I hate that you were alone and running so long? Yes. But I can't say that I'm not grateful for it because, baby. I think it was bringing you right to me."

I was crying again, listening to him, different tears. Healing tears.

"From the moment you backed up into me in that school office, and I felt you? When I looked over at Monica and saw the way she was smiling at you and looked at me? I knew that was it. You were mine. It was done and there wouldn't be any more looking for me. You're not stupid, Rebecca Wareman. You are brave and strong and amazing. I would go through hell for you. I'll be your punching bag and sounding board no matter how many times you need me to be. This relationship isn't always going to be pretty, but it's ours and I'm never letting go. I love you."

I sniffled again, "I love you too." I looked up at him and he grinned down at me.

"Do you at least feel better?" he asked softly, running his thumb over my cheek gently, cupping it and searching my eyes with his gray ones.

I nodded, leaning up and kissing the tip of his nose, like we often did to each other.

He kissed the tip of my nose in return and picked up my glasses from my lap, setting them up on the kitchen bar from the floor where we sat.

Glancing around the kitchen with slightly blurry eyes I groaned at the wrapping paper, tape and scissors that had sprawled across the floor. At least the presents had stayed on top.

He chuckled, squeezing me tight again.

"You're quite the firecracker when you get worked up," he said, jokingly.

"Shut up." I grumbled, half-heartedly, still feeling worn out from my emotional release.

"You do know how much I love and adore you right?" he asked.

Looking up at him, I nodded again.

"How much I need you day in and day out? There's only you, Becks. From now until forever. There's only you," he said, cupping the side of my face again, his eyes boring into mine with intensity.

"I know," I whispered, "There's only you for me too."

His lips met mine, gently pressing, and I sighed into him, wrapping my arms around his neck to draw him closer against me. He tilted his head, deepening the kiss, running his tongue across the seam of my lips so I parted them for him. His tongue delved inside my mouth, coaxing mine to dance with his as the feelings within the room shifted. Moving his right hand down my back he guided me down to the floor, following until he was braced over me, never breaking our contact.

I didn't care that the wood was hard under my back when Lucas' heat was pressing into me from above. I felt like I needed this closeness with him after the explosion and apparently he did too. His hands ran down my sides gently, up under my sweatshirt, until he covered my breasts, squeezing gently.

"Is this okay?" he whispered, lips moving against mine. Always checking in with me. Always making sure everything was alright.

"More than," I whispered back as he massaged my breasts

through the lace of my bra before he took my mouth in another heated, searing kiss. His rough fingertips found my hardened nipples through the lace, flicking softly as my back arched and I moaned softly into his mouth. His thumb and pointer finger on each hand pinched my nipples gently, twisting them.

I felt my core pulse with need as wetness pooled between my thighs and I whispered his name, breathlessly.

"You're always so ready for me," he murmured against my neck, licking and sucking at it. "So responsive. How wet are you already?" he questioned, biting my skin softly.

His mouth was going to actually set me on fire one day. I was instantly desperate for him. I needed him inside me, just so I could feel him and know he was there and mine forever.

"Lucas, I need you." I whispered, threading my fingers through his hair and tugging until his gray eyes met my brown ones. His eyes darkened at whatever he saw there.

"I've got you, baby. I've always got you." he said. Lucas rose to his knees over me, gently pulling me up to remove my sweatshirt and bra. His large hand pressed into my chest so I laid back down on the floor.

I shivered at the cold, my nipples tightening further. He leaned over me, covering one of them with his mouth and laving at the bud with his tongue, sucking.

I cried out into the empty kitchen, arching against his mouth as he switched to the other side, treating it to the same attention.

"Lucas," my hips were moving restlessly under him, desperate for his touch.

"Shhhh," he hushed me softly. He was running his hands down and sliding my leggings and panties off, tossing them over his shoulder. He looked like a dark god in the light of the kitchen as he reached behind his neck and pulled his shirt off. My body heated further as my eyes took him in. Every inch from his neck down was covered in ink and I licked my lips. My dark god.

He unbuckled his belt slowly, drawing out the tension, unbuttoning then unzipping his jeans.

"Lucas, please," I begged. I didn't care thatI was pleading. He was torturing me.

Placing his left hand beside my head, he leaned over me, taking my mouth in another heated kiss. His right hand moved down my chest between my breasts and over my stomach. When his fingers touched the apex of my thighs I parted for him automatically, desperate for his touch.

His fingertips slid over the slick collection of my arousal between my legs, moving over my lower lips as he groaned.

CHAPTER TEN
LUCAS

"**F**uck. You're soaked," I groaned against Becks' soft, plump lips as my fingers glided over her pussy. Lifting my head, I looked down, sitting back on my knees slightly so I could see. The inside of her thighs glistened under the lighting in the kitchen and I let my forehead meet hers again.

"Jesus. You're desperate for it, aren't you?" I murmured as she panted under me, nodding frantically.

"I need you." Her husky voice was going to be the end of me.

I shifted the wrist of my right hand, using two fingers to part her gently, slowly sliding my middle finger inside her to the knuckle. I watched her arch her head back, mouth falling open on a moan and I growled softly, beginning to pump it in and out of her.

"Lucas, yes!" she cried out, open in her need for me, uninhibited knowing that we were alone in the house. "I need more,

I need you," she begged again.

It was almost my breaking point, but she was going to come before I took her.

I slid another finger into her, moving my hand faster as her hips undulated against me. I could hear how wet she was when my fingers exited and entered her and it drove me harder knowing she was desperate for me.

"Can you take another one?" I rasped out, kissing at her lips as she whimpered.

"Yes, please. Take me, do whatever, I need you!" she cried out.

I fucking loved this side of her. Adding a third finger she groaned at the stretch as I rapidly started fucking her with my hand.

"You going to come for me, sweet girl?" I asked looking down into her chocolate eyes, her face flushed and breasts heaving as she panted.

"Yes," she nodded, frantic, "Oh God, Lucas -"

"I know what you need," I answered, moving my thumb to her clit and pressing into it firmly, rubbing in circles as my fingers continued to pump into her. I watched her eyes lose focus with pleasure as her lips parted.

She arched up, shoving her pussy against my hand, thighs trembling as she let go. She convulsed around my fingers, her pussy trying to keep them inside, and I let her ride her orgasm out until every ounce of pleasure was wrung out of her.

She panted under me, fingernails embedded into my shoulder, just how I liked them. I waited until her eyes met mine again before I reached down, taking my hardened cock out. It was painfully hard, leaking precum from the tip.

Rubbing it through the soaked, glistening folds of her pussy, I groaned, torturing myself further.

Her hands wrapped around my neck, fingers linking at the back as she gazed up at me, eyes full of love.

"Take me," she whispered. "I'm yours. Forever."

That's all I needed to hear. I moved both hands to brace against the floor beside her head, sliding inside her inch-by-inch as she opened and stretched around me.

"God, baby. Every time just makes it feel even more right." I murmured, looking down at her. "You keep those beautiful brown eyes on me." I said, pressing in with my hips until our pelvises met.

"You're mine." I gasped, hair falling across my forehead, sweat beading on my brow.

"I'm yours," she echoed, "And you're mine. You're my everything, Lucas," she whispered, staring up at me.

I started moving in and out of her at a steady pace, her inching up across the floor with every rock of our bodies, me following her, desperate to remain inside of her. I'd follow her straight into the depths of hell. I growled with the emotion in the moment and kissed her hard as she wrapped her arms and legs around me tight, holding on like she'd never let go.

"You feel so fucking perfect around me." I said against her mouth, both of us panting. "You're so tight and hot and wet." I worked my hips faster as she cried out, hitting that spot inside her that made her come apart for me.

Moving my right hand off the floor, I gripped her neck, squeezing gently.

"Open those eyes," I said when they fluttered shut, her mouth parted. I could feel her clenching around my cock, spasming, and knew she was close again. Driving my hips in harder the sounds of our fucking echoed through the kitchen. "I want them on me when you come. You say my name when you come around my cock, Rebecca. You hear me?"

She was nodding frantically, practically sobbing.

"Yes. Please, Lucas. Oh -"

"That's it. You're doing so well. Taking me perfectly." I kept squeezing my hand around her pretty throat reflexively, syncing with her pussy squeezing my cock inside. "Come for me, sweetheart. Look at me and show me how good I make you feel."

Her eyes widened and her neck arched as her nails dug into my back. I fucking hoped she drew blood. I'd get the marks tattooed this time, to mark this night. I felt her pussy clamp down as I drove into her one more time and we both fell off the edge together coming hard as she yelled my name through the house.

Keeping my hips pressed into hers and my cock deep inside her, I kissed her while we were both breathless and panting, still holding her neck, letting her milk my cock as she shook.

Resting my forehead against hers, I kissed the tip of her nose and whispered, "I love you, more than my own life."

"I love you too," she responded, holding me tightly against her.

"Mom? Dad?" Nat's voice made me sit straight up in our king-sized bed, sunlight streaming through the windows and skylight. I blinked at the clock to clear my vision and saw it read ten-thirty a.m. *Fuck*. Monica and the girls had started decorating and setting up the books around eight this morning. . I slept through the entire morning and so had Becks. My eyes moved over at her, sprawled on her stomach, head under her pillow, dark hair down in a riot of waves. I heard her grumble and snorted.

"Baby, it's closer to afternoon than morning and Nat's home." I said, voice raspy with sleep.

Becks jerked up from under the pillow looking deliciously rumpled and blinked at me owlishly.

"What?" she murmured.

"We slept in. Nat is home. It's Christmas Eve." Poking at her side I made a mental note to set an alarm next time so I could take her in the morning sunlight before our daughter got home.

"Oh my God! Lucas, we're naked! Don't let her come in here."

I threw my head back laughing as she rolled out of bed and scrambled naked into the bathroom.

"Baby, you've had the talk with Nat. I'm pretty sure she knows what we get up to in here, let alone when she's out of the house."

Becks walked out scowling at me, tightening the robe clinging to her body, hair falling over her shoulder.

"Still! Put some pants on. Monica is with her." She reached down grabbing a pair of my pajama pants from the floor and threw them at me, hitting me directly in the face.

"Whoops," she giggled.

"You'll pay for that later." I muttered, watching her leave the room.

"Nat, good morning, sweetheart! We overslept." I heard her voice greeting our daughter and stood, slipping my pants on.

"Busy night?" I heard Monica's teasing voice and laughed to myself before padding out and down the hall to the kitchen. Meeting Monica's eyes behind Becks' back, I raised my eyebrows questioningly.

She nodded, grinning wide as Becks hugged the girls and reached for her. They were going to get on the road to head to her parents and then Paul's today.

"I love you all. Drive safe and text me when you get there," she said. "Do you need anything to drink or eat on the way?"

"Becks, we're covered. I'll text when we're there. They only live an hour away."

Monica's parents and Paul's family had moved to a smaller, more rural retirement type of community that was just an hour's drive away from us.

Monica winked at me and left with her girls.

I grabbed my hoodie from the hook by the back door and glanced out the window. It hadn't snowed overnight and while the ground was still white, the path I'd made to the shed was still clear. Turning I saw Nat grinning at me excitedly, still bundled in her coat, my wife fixing a mug of coffee with her back to us, completely unaware.

"Can we?" Nat whispered.

I nodded. We had a big day planned tomorrow with all our friends going to Nan's to spend Christmas. We could have our family Christmas on Christmas Eve and start our own traditions.

"Can you what?" Becks turned around, looking at us suspiciously.

"Slip on some shoes and a coat, babe. Nat and I wanna give you your Christmas present."

Becks blinked at me.

"And I need shoes and a coat?" she repeated, blinking at me behind her glasses.

"Yep." Nat started giggling.

"What did you all do?" muttered Becks, walking into the front hall and getting her coat and snow boots.

"We're gonna have our Christmas on Christmas Eve." Nat was bouncing with excitement, following Becks like a little girl, instead of the teenager she was. She practically vibrated with anticipation and energy.

Becks looked over at her, raising her eyebrows.

"Dad said we could. It would be our new family tradition!" Nat finished.

Becks' eyes filled with tears and she nodded, hugging Nat tightly and looking at me over her shoulder.

This first Christmas was going to be an emotional one for sure.

"I don't think I'll ever get tired of hearing her call you dad." Becks said, releasing Nat to run ahead of us and sneak into the shed to record everything.

"You're telling me. In some ways it seems so natural like she's been here and done it my whole life. In other ways I can't believe I have a daughter." I said, slightly choked-up myself.

I slung my arm over Becks' shoulder and guided her through the kitchen and out the back door.

Her brown eyes scanned the backyard, not finding Nat.

"Where's Nat? What did you all do?" she asked, the suspicion slowly trying to grow into trepidation.

"Just relax and let it happen, beautiful. Let me spoil you. This is how it always should've been for you."

Her eyes met mine, looking up at me as I ushered her down

the path through the backyard to the old beat up building.

You couldn't tell the inside was a beautiful library from the outside and Becks gave me a questioning look. I stood her right in front of the door and faced her. Leaning down I kissed the tip of her nose.

"You stand right here. Keep those eyes closed. Do not open them until I tell you to," I ordered. "You'll ruin the surprise and Nat will be devastated."

Her eyes rolled, but she shut them, and I opened the door leading into the library. Seeing Nat with her big blue eyes hopping up and down. Everything looked perfect. I turned and grabbed both of Becks' hands, leading her a couple steps forward until she was in the room.

Backing up, I stood by Nat and looked at my beautiful fiancee, completely oblivious to what we'd done for her. I looked down.

"You recording?" I asked quietly.

Nat nodded, "Ever since you opened the door."

"Alright, Peanut. Here we go," I said just for her to hear, before raising my voice, "Open your eyes, Rebecca."

CHAPTER ELEVEN

BECKS

I sighed at Lucas and Nat's antics and opened my eyes, scanning the room as they came into focus and adjusting to the scene that lay before me.

Lucas and Nat yelled in unison, "Merry Christmas!"

I gasped, the breath completely stolen from me. How had they managed this? My hands covered my mouth as I took several more steps into the room and turned in a slow circle.

Beautiful hardwood floor covered with some comfy area rugs, a mini fridge and coffee bar. A comfy chair and lounge. Art prints framed with my favorite fictional locations alongside pictures of my family and friends.

Books. So many books spread out over shelves that covered every bare part of the wall.

There were fairy lights and dim lighting creating a calming atmosphere. There was even a neon sign strung up proclaiming this was "Becks' Library".

Bookish merchandise was scattered among the shelves and everywhere I looked was another perfect detail and it was utterly overwhelming.

"Breathe," I felt Lucas' hands on my arms and took a deep shuddering breath in.

"How?" I whispered "It's too much."

"It's nothing." Lucas scoffed. "Those extra night shifts, I was out here building this. Laying the floor and painting and building shelves. I had stuff shipped to the station and Nick and Trevor helped me smuggle it in. I owe Nick big because he'd drive me here from the station so my truck was there," he laughed and continued, "It's not too much. It's everything you deserve and more. Nat helped me. Monica and her girls helped me. You deserved a special space, Becks. Somewhere quiet to just be, baby."

Tears were pouring off of my face and I was shaking as I walked forward, taking in the shelves, each book, each piece of merchandise, the blankets strewn about.

My favorite coffee and ingredients stocked the bar and I opened the mini fridge to more snacks and drinks that I Lucas had learned were my favorites.

"I picked out all the books on these shelves," Nat announced, grabbing my hand and pulling me over to a specific shelf, "They're books I remembered you loved but would never keep. I remembered you checking them out or finding everywhere we went. Dad even found a few that were signed by the author."

She was grinning, but looking at me unsure, probably because I was a snotty, sobbing mess.

"Nat, it's absolutely perfect. Thank you, sweet girl." I wrapped my arms around my baby and hugged her tightly to me, still in shock.

"The outside is going to be redone this summer," Lucas added, watching us. "Make it pretty to look at out there too." He stepped forward, handing me a keychain with one key on it. The keychain read, "Beck's Library" and had books stamped on it.

"I feel like nothing I say is going to convey what I'm feeling," I murmured, still gawking around the library.

"You don't have to say anything," he soothed, his own voice gruff with emotion as he watched us. "You deserve the world. If I could get the moon for you I would."

Nat giggled and rolled her eyes.

"You never settle for anything less than this, Peanut," he added. "You find a man that will strive to give you the world too. You deserve it. Both of you."

I was bawling again, not sure if I'd ever actually stopped. Lucas walked forward and hugged us both to him. His girls.

"How did you get all this so perfectly decorated?" I asked again.

"Monica, her girls, and Nat came over around eight this morning to place all the books and decor," he grinned and I gasped. "I wasn't expecting to oversleep and still be in bed the entire time," he added a little sheepishly.

"You must've been sleeping real good if you were that worn out," said Nat, walking off oblivious to what we had gotten up to last night that had kept us up so late.

I blushed and Lucas laughed, kissing the top of my head.

"Nat and I will go in and fix some lunch, then we can open the rest of the presents," Lucas suggested.

Nat nodded eagerly, moving to follow him back into the house.

"There better not be anything else for me!" I warned.

"Nothing I did could even compare to this." I murmured to myself, lifting my arms up and dropping them, feeling overwhelmed and self-conscious.

"Nat, run on into the house and get your bag unpacked and relax until I get in. Give us a few minutes, yeah?" asked Lucas, keeping his eyes on me.

"Okay. I'll call Lexi and tell her," she squealed and took off.

Lucas watched until she got into the house and shut the door to the shed. Walking over to me he gripped my chin between his fingers and tilted my face up to him.

"You listen to me, Rebecca Wareman," he whispered with authority lacing his voice.

My eyes were wide, looking up at him.

"You don't owe me shit. You don't have to give me something in return just because I did something for you. That's not a relationship. That's not any kind of relationship. This is love. I did it because I wanted to. My gift is seeing you filled with joy and getting to love you every goddamn day of our lives and beyond. My gift is that little girl out there you brought into my life and let me be a father to. You don't owe me anything."

Then his lips were on mine, devouring, his fingers threading through my still loose hair and pulling it back until my neck was arched as he kissed down it.

"Lucas," I said breathlessly "Nat -"

"Will be on the fucking phone with Lexi and Lacey for an hour if we let her," he growled, pushing me back against a bookshelf as my body heated. He tugged at the belt closing my robe, letting it fall open and shoved my coat off my shoulders.

His eyes heated as he took in my body, bare before him under the blue satin fabric of the robe he'd bought me months ago. He leaned down, sucking a hardened nipple into his mouth and drawing on it, causing me to cry out, my hands on his shoulders, fingernails digging into his hoodie.

"Better stay quiet," he murmured, "This shed isn't sound-proof."

He continued suckling at my nipple before moving over to the other one, nipping at it. His hand delved between my thighs finding me soaked for him, as always.

"Lucas," I gasped again. "We can't-"

"Oh, baby girl. We can and we're gonna," he growled, standing up to his full height and pushing his pajama pants down to his ankles. His cock sprang free, drops of pre-cum leaking from the tip, and I looked at him whimpering softly. Pressing into my body with his, he lifted my right leg, wrapping it around his hip, guiding his cock to my wet folds and pressing in, bending his knees to angle into me.

"Better hold on," he warned, voice low, my arms coming around his shoulders tighter as he took my mouth again. Kissing me deeper before thrusting all the way inside of me.

I cried out, the noise swallowed by his kiss as his hips started snapping back and forth quickly. My back pressing into the bookshelves behind me, causing a bite of pain, but adding to the pleasure of the suddenness of the moment and knowing he needed me this badly.

He ground his hips against mine, reaching between us and rubbing my clit with two of his fingers as he looked down between us.

"Look at us," he demanded, "Look how perfectly you take me, Rebecca. Look how you were fucking made for me."

I looked down where we were joined, watching his cock slicked with my wetness entering and exiting me and everything rushed over me. The emotions of this morning, the movement of his hips and fingers. How he looked, brow tightened as he focused on getting me to finish before him. Still in his hoodie, pajama pants around his ankles. Me in my open robe. In my new library.

I clenched around him, groaning softly, already close.

"Lucas-" I breathed out.

"That's right. You're gonna come for me, Rebecca. All over me. Take everything, baby."

He drove harder and faster against me and I practically screamed as his mouth covered mine and I orgasmed around him, milking him as he moaned into my mouth and followed.

We stood, him inside me, foreheads against each other, panting, our chests heaving, and he looked at me, brushing my hair off my forehead.

"I love you. So fucking much it hurts sometimes." he promised.

"I love you the same way." I pulled his head down kissing him softly.

He pulled back and slid from my body, smiling at the sight of his come leaking out of me. His large hands closed my robe, tying it, before leaning down and pulling his pajamas up.

"You enjoy your library for a while. Nat and I are gonna fix lunch."

Like he hadn't just given me the gift of all gifts with a side of orgasm against the bookshelves.

I snorted in disbelief of the scenario and he leaned down kissing the tip of my nose.

"Enjoy it, Rebecca" he whispered, then he turned and left, shutting the door behind him and leaving me in my own library.

I immediately looked around again, my hands still trembling from the surprise, emotions, and orgasm. I pulled my cell phone out of my pocket and dialed one number.

"Did you cry?" Monica's voice was filled with levity. I could hear Lexi and Lacey speaking to Nat on the phone in the background.

"You are a brat!" I exclaimed, bursting into tears again.

"Aw, Becks. You deserve everything. ll the good things," she said, sounding tearful herself.

"So do you," I whispered.

"We need to have a wine and book night soon," she added. "I was drooling over that library this morning before we left to wake you and sleepy-head up."

I blushed even though she couldn't see me and snorted.

"Thank you, Monica." I said, running my hand over a bookshelf lovingly.

"You're welcome, Rebecca," she replied. "I love you. I'll text you when we get there and see you tomorrow."

"Okay."

Hanging up I shot a text off to Trevor and Nick to thank them for all their help as well.

> Thank you all for the help you did with my Christmas present.
>
> Trevor
>
> Hey, anything for friends. Merry Christmas, Becks. :)
>
> Nick
>
> You are welcome, because you're pretty. Lucas owes me. Merry Christmas, B.

I laughed at their responses and shook my head. Pulling one of my favorite books off of the shelf, I sat in the overstuffed chair and opened it, gasping when I saw it was signed by the author. I ran my fingertips over the signature, tears dripping off of my face again, and I snuggled down to read.

"Family meeting in the living room!"

Tossing the used towel in the laundry room off the kitchen, I walked over, peeking around the corner at Lucas standing in front of the Christmas tree.

"Family meeting?" I asked, quirking an eyebrow.

"I didn't stutter," he stated, grinning with his hands on his hips. "Get in here."

"What am I grounded, daddy?" I sassed and watched his gray eyes darken, arms crossing in front of his chest. He took a step towards me just as Nat burst into the room.

"We'll table that for later," he spoke, his eyes promising me what he couldn't say.

"Am I in trouble?" Nat asked plopping down on the couch.

"No one is in trouble. You all have guilty consciences," laughed Lucas.

"What's going on then?" I sat by my daughter wrapping an arm around her shoulders, even as she made a face at me.

"We need to talk to Nat about the things that have been bothering you lately and triggering you too, Becks." Lucas spoke seriously now gauging my reaction. "She's old enough to know things have happened that have made her mom anxious and it's been worse lately."

My head turned, meeting my daughter's blue eyes even as she was nodding in agreement.

"How can we make it better?" she asked, head tilted.

Blowing out a breath, I leaned back, letting my head fall onto the back of the couch.

"None of that," came Lucas' voice, "things need to change."

I straightened again, staring at both of them.

"You all aren't doing anything wrong on purpose."

"We know, Mom. But we want to help make things easier. So you're not … what's that word?"

"Triggered, Peanut," Lucas nodded.

"You've talked about this?" I asked, meeting Lucas' eyes.

He nodded, watching, still gauging my reaction.

Sighing, I conceded.

"The only thing is the messes," I began softly, "It's not a big deal to normal people…"

"Hey," Lucas scolded sternly. He shook his head as he spoke, "none of that."

I felt my cheeks heat, "Clark…he didn't let me clean." I scrubbed my hands over my face. "I know. A grown adult. But he made me live in filth. It was part of his mental mind games. It's just little things. Putting things back where they go, putting dirty clothes in the hamper, wiping cabinets down? I know it's so silly. But it just…it messes with me so badly."

Nat's small hands covered mine, where I had unconsciously started picking at my fingernails.

"Mom. It's ok." She said, sounding wise beyond her years. "I'll try to do better. I promise."

"For that matter, I will too." Lucas added. "And we need to

start being open with each other instead of staying quiet about what bothers us. These family meetings can be called by anyone. Anytime. Day or night. We're a unit. A family. We love and care about each other. We have to communicate."

I was just staring at them both through a film of tears. Why was I always crying lately? I made things so much harder on myself than they needed to be.

"Thank you." I spoke softly, my voice shaking. "I'll try to be better about speaking up when something's bothering me instead of just holding it in until I snap. I love you both more than anything else."

"We love you too, Mom." Nat replied wrapping her arms around me tightly as Lucas smiled at me.

"Open it! Open it!"

Lucas was being as loud as Nat at this point. She was working on opening her presents in our cozy living room. The snow had started again and cast a picturesque atmosphere behind the lit Christmas tree.

He had never gotten to experience a Christmas morning through the eyes of a parent and he was relishing it. He kept looking at me like an eager puppy and my stomach got butter-flies watching him dote on our little girl.

She'd gotten a new pair of sneakers she'd been asking for for months, knee pads for volleyball, a cell phone case, and several gift cards. Practically breathless with overstimulation and Lucas' antics she'd worked her way to the last small box that I didn't remember wrapping. I looked at Lucas with an eyebrow raised and he just shook his head at me.

Nat's fingers worked in a frenzy through the wrapping paper and revealed a white box. Opening the lid, she gasped, and immediately burst into tears.

"Nat! Honey?" I laughed, walking over to where she sat and wrapping my arm around her. I looked inside the box and immediately understood.

Inside lay two blue cat collars, complete with little bells on them. She'd begged for a feline friend for as long as I could remember. We'd never been able to have one with all the picking up and running throughout the years.

Lucas and I had talked about adopting a pair of kittens someday, both okay with the idea, and apparently her dad had chosen this as her Christmas surprise.

"Oh, sweetheart," I laughed softly, kissing the top of her head.

"Do you like it? I have an in at the animal shelter through animal control. They said we could stop in tomorrow night and look at the kittens then, with no one else around."

Nat just stood up and threw herself into his arms.

I watched my little girl soaking up all the love this man had to give us and got teary again myself.

They'd fixed a wonderful Christmas Eve lunch of boxed macaroni and cheese and came and got me from my cozy library when it was ready.

Locking it up and giving it an unbelieving shake of my head I'd followed them back in to eat. Afterwards we took turns opening our presents. Lucas was last to go and he only had a few.

One from me and one from Natasha. There was an envelope

for him on the tree that he had no idea about from both of us. When it was his turn, after watching his girls open their presents Natasha was practically vibrating with anticipation again.

He was overzealous about the "World's #1 Dad" travel mug that Natasha had gotten him and even got a little misty-eyed himself.

I'd given him a watch that I'd seen him looking at months before, that he passed by because he said his old one worked just fine. Lucas scolded me thoroughly for it, to Natasha's delight, and I put him in place when I reminded me he'd gifted me a fully furnished library.

"We have something else for you, Dad." Natasha walked to the Christmas tree and grabbed the envelope nestled in its branches. Smiling softly at me I returned the grin and watched her present it to him suddenly shy.

My hand covered my mouth because I was already near tears. We'd talked about this and I knew he wanted to do it, but we hadn't bitten the bullet yet.

"What else could you all have given me that I don't already have?" Lucas joked.

"Just open it." Nat said, even more quietly now.

Lucas' gray eyes met hers a little worriedly as his finger slid along the envelope, opening it slowly.

I kept telling myself I was not going to cry again.

Unfolding the small stack of papers, Lucas froze and I watched this six-foot-six man, covered in tattoos, dissolve into full-blown tears himself.

Natasha had handwritten a single question on the first page, *You already let me call you Dad. Can we make it official?*

I went and had all the paperwork drawn up as we'd been

working on it together for a while. He had been so unsuspecting that I'd done everything and all he'd have to do is sign along the dotted line.

Nat was crying.

I was crying.

Lucas was crying.

"Yes, Peanut. Of course I want to make it official in every single way we can."

Nat jumped into his lap and they held each other while he smiled at me tearfully over her head.

My heart felt full, warm, and a weight seemed to roll off my shoulders.

Somehow, in that single moment, everything felt settled and more peaceful than it had in a long time.

Lucas kissed the top of Natasha's head and stood, walking over to me, pulling me up to stand with him. Then he dipped me back and kissed me in front of our tree as Nat yelled gross and hid behind the pillow.

Everything was as it should be

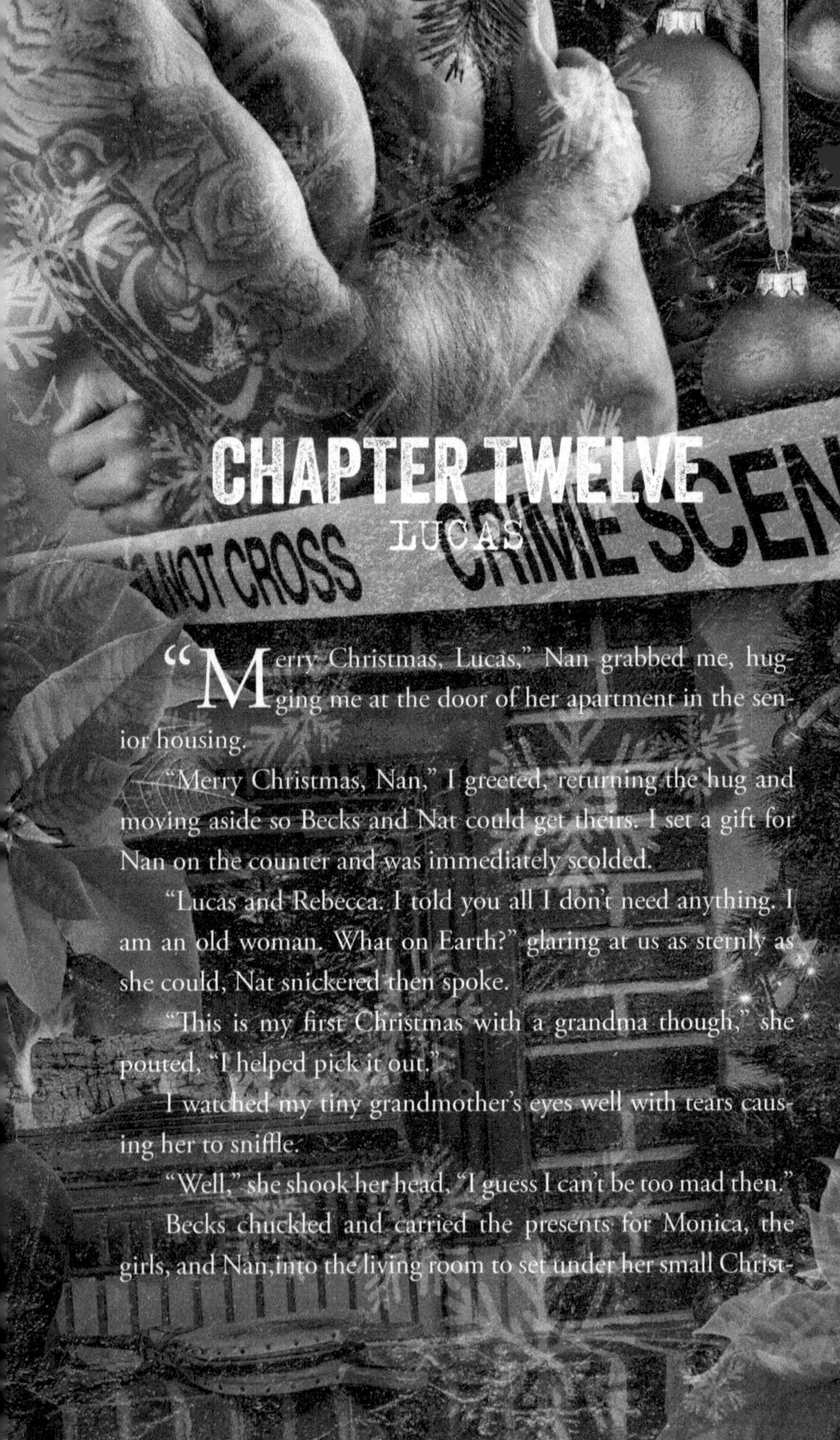

CHAPTER TWELVE

LUCAS

"Merry Christmas, Lucas," Nan grabbed me, hugging me at the door of her apartment in the senior housing.

"Merry Christmas, Nan," I greeted, returning the hug and moving aside so Becks and Nat could get theirs. I set a gift for Nan on the counter and was immediately scolded.

"Lucas and Rebecca. I told you all I don't need anything. I am an old woman. What on Earth?" glaring at us as sternly as she could, Nat snickered then spoke.

"This is my first Christmas with a grandma though," she pouted, "I helped pick it out."

I watched my tiny grandmother's eyes well with tears causing her to sniffle.

"Well," she shook her head, "I guess I can't be too mad then."

Becks chuckled and carried the presents for Monica, the girls, and Nan, into the living room to set under her small Christmas tree.

"Everything smells so good, Vi!" she cooed, standing to take off her coat.

"Now! Young lady. I've told you to call me grandma or nan just like everyone else."

"Okay, Nan. I'm sorry." Beck's eyes sparkled at her feisty tone. "Nat, can you run these coats to the guest room and lay them on the bed?" she asked softly.

Nat was up and off within a blink.

"How was your all's first Christmas then?" asked Nan, shuffling to the stove to check on the food.

"Wonderful " Becks and I answered in unison.

"Jinx. You owe me a coke!" Becks laughed.

"Did you like your surprise?" Nan stood, her knowing eyes sparkling.

"You knew?" Becks accused, trying to sound affronted.

"Well, of course."

"Is there anyone who didn't?" Becks' asked shoving me lightly. "How on Earth did you all manage to keep it a secret?"

"I have my ways." I answered, slinging an arm around her and pulling her close. "That library is absolutely nothing compared to the gift you and Nat gave me."

"Oh?" said Nan, distracted with something in the fridge now. "What did they get you?"

"Nat's adoption papers. All I have to do is sign and file them. Then I'm her legal father."

Nan jerked upright, nearly hitting her head on the fridge's ceiling, eyes full of tears again.

"Oh, Lucas," she murmured. "Rebecca, that is the best gift you could have given either of us this Christmas."

Becks sniffled again and mumbled, "Dammit, I'm always crying lately." even as my tiny grandmother drew her in for a tight, lingering hug.

"Nan. Did they tell you you're gonna be my official Nan now?" asked Nat sliding back into the room.

"Slow down." scolded Nan. "And yes, beautiful. They did." she drew Nat in for a tight hug herself and smiled at me over her head. "Your Papa would be so proud of you, Lucas."

I nodded, clearing my throat.

"Dammit." I grumbled to myself.

Becks laughed, poking me when there was a knock on the door behind us.

Running to open it we heard Nat squeal"Merry Christmas, Lexi!"

"I'm here too." growled Lacey, predictably.

"Don't start," came Monica's tired voice.

"Gangs all here." I laughed as Becks ran to greet them herself.

"Congratulations, Dad." whispered Nan, wrapping an arm around my waist and looking up at me proudly.

"Thanks, Nan." I whispered softly, smiling down at the tiny woman that had raised me to be the man I was today.

"Vi, that was amazing. You truly outdid yourself." Monica said, sitting back in her chair.

Lacey, Lexi, and Nat had finished their meal and were in the living room watching a Christmas movie.

"It truly was amazing." Added Becks. "I would love to come over and have you show me your recipes sometime. Spend the day together."

Nan smiled warmly at her, "I'd like that, Becks. It was no trouble. Usually I'm just cooking for Lucas and myself. This was enjoyable. Having a brood to cook for. Everything is so convenient now."

I snorted, looking at all the disposable pans and dishware she'd used.

"Easy clean-up." I nodded. "You're such a modern woman, Nan."

"Don't be a smart ass, Lucas." Nan sassed as I choked.

"Nan, language."

"I'm in my eighties, Lucas, not a nun."

Monica and Becks were laughing hysterically at this point, looking adoringly at the feisty little woman.

"Shall we open presents?" asked Nan. "Even Lacey looked excited. It's been so long since I've watched children open presents."

Monica smiled at her fondly, "Of course. We'll help you with the easy clean-up after."

Following my shuffling Nan into the living room we all took empty seats as the girls took turns playing Santa. Soon the room was filled with wrapping paper and laughter. Exclamations of surprise and adoration.

Nan had a fit over the new flatscreen television Becks and I had gotten her, knowing hers was on its last legs and from the 80s. She even grew teary again at Nat's coffee mug that said "Greatest Great-Nan".

She'd given each of the girls a scarf and hat set she'd knitted herself. Each seemed to understand the love that had gone into such a gift.

Monica and Becks had each gotten one too, Becks getting misty-eyed yet again. These women and their tears. I was beginning to understand what Paul had always talked about, being outnumbered.

I had to shake my head at the fact that he'd left me here with all of them, remembering a long ago conversation.

I looked around at my tiny family that had come together so perfectly and smiled at my blessings. Leaving Nan to visit with Mon and Becks I snuck into the kitchen to clean up and throw things away.

Nan came shuffling in after a few minutes, scolding me for doing all the work.

"You cooked for us Nan," I countered, "It was the least I could do. If you hadn't gotten in my face when you did, I may have never been a cop. I may have never been who I am and who I need to be to deserve Rebecca and that little girl out there. This is the least I could do."

Feeling sentimental myself suddenly and a little overwhelmed at the emotions that came with a first Christmas with a family.

Also the first Christmas, in a long time, without my best friend.

Nan just patted my arm, drawing me down into a hug, like she understood. Just like she always had as I'd been growing up.

"You deserve all this and more, sweet boy," she assured me softly. "You may be bigger than me now, and all tatted up, but I'm still your Nan," she said a little more feisty to break the mood.

I laughed at her. "I know Nan. I wouldn't have it any other way."

Later after we'd cleaned up, had dessert, and watched a Christmas movie together. We said our good-bye's and I-love-you's.

"Thank you for inviting me and the girls over tonight." said Monica softly, standing by her car.

Lexi, Lacey, and Nat were hugging and chattering goodbye behind us.

"It means a lot. It's been different this year," she said, trailing off, her eyes seeming to shimmer in the streetlight.

I scooped her into a big hug. "Any time, Mon. I'm always here for you and the girls."

She returned my hug, patting my back. Stepping aside she hugged Becks tightly and told her she loved her.

"I love you too, Mon. Merry Christmas." said Becks softly, handing her a small package.

"Becks!" said Monica, exasperated.

We'd already given the girls their gifts inside, but Rebecca had wanted to do this privately, unsure of how Monica would react. I knew she'd love it but Becks was so nervous about anything regarding this. I'd helped her with it and made it happen knowing it would mean the world to Monica.

Opening the box, she gasped, immediately denying.

"Becks, Lucas, I can't accept this." she exclaimed, looking at the sapphire ring in a white gold setting. "It looks expensive."

"It's yours," said Becks. "From us and Paul."

Monica's head jerked up, meeting my eyes, then Becks'.

"What?" she whispered.

"I used some of his ashes you gave me" I said gruffly. "They're in the stone. Becks had Paul's badge number engraved on the inside along with 'Firecracker' for what he called you."

Tears were streaming down Monica's face and Beck's too again. The girls were watching, wide-eyed and quiet.

Monica slipped the ring on her finger and it fit perfectly.

"How did you know the size?" she asked, sniffling.

"Paul." I murmured.

Her eyes swung up to mine then Becks' questioningly.

"He gave us your ring size. In case something ever happened. He said to make you a piece of jewelry. He left the design to Lucas' or my discretion. But he wanted sapphire and white gold. He even had money in the envelope to pay for half." Becks' broke off sniffling. "It was for the first holiday or occasion after….if something happened."

Monica covered her face, crying freely now.

"I let Becks' design it, and really thank God she's here now. Can you imagine what it would've looked like if I'd tried to do that on my own?" I joked, trying to lighten the mood. "I don't know what Paul was thinking, leaving me with that kind of responsibility before he knew Becks would be around."

Monica snorted and tossed her head back laughing through her tears.

"That's just something Paul would do." she giggled. "Make you panic as one of his damn jokes."

Becks laughed and stepped forward hugging her tight again.

"I love you, Mon." she whispered.

"I love you too." Monica returned.

CHAPTER THIRTEEN

BECKS

"Merry Christmas, sweetheart." I whispered, leaning down and kissing Nat's forehead.

"Love you, Peanut." said Lucas, behind me, smiling down at our daughter.

"Merry Christmas, I love you both too." answered our daughter, smiling up at us from where she sat on her bed. Two kittens curled up to her side were purring softly and she was looking at them adoringly, already lost in love with them. We'd swung by to meet Lucas' friend at the animal shelter after leaving Nan's and here we were. Grandparents to kittens.

Both black kittens with little white socks on their feet. The little boys were siblings. Lucas had made a joke that he finally had more testosterone in the house.

Nat was still thinking of names but had everything set up for them and was claiming she was ready to take responsibility. They were cute and it was fun to watch Lucas melting over baby animals the way he was.

Shutting the door to Nat's room I followed my fiance down the stairs to the living room. The only light was coming from the Christmas tree and the snow was falling gently outside the window.

"I know you hate it, but wow." I said, gesturing to the view.

Lucas looked over at me, "It's okay I guess. It is Christmas, after all."

I poked him in the side as he wrapped his arms around me, drawing me close to him.

"This was pretty good for our First Christmas, wasn't it?" I whispered.

"It was the best Christmas I've ever had." he answered, kissing me softly.

Merry
Christmas

THE END

Be on the lookout for Monica and Trevor's second-chance romance, *"Fourteen Years"* in Book Two of the Finding Freedom series by D. Raven.

Coming April 2025.

Need More Becks and Lucas?
Wondering how they met?

Check out Lucas and Beck's Story in *"Thirteen Years"* Book One of the Finding Freedom series by D. Raven.

Released July 2024.

ACKNOWLEDGEMENTS AND THANK YOUS

What I thought would be one book with Thirteen Years has grown so much. This novella was unexpected, but Lucas and Becks were not done with me... and they're still not. I'll just leave you all to ponder that.

It's looking like this series is going to end up being three books and four or five novellas. So brace yourselves.

Thank you again to Izzy Elliott/A.E.C., for continuing to publish me, encourage me, and inspire me with everything that you are. You are the sister I always wanted but didn't know how desperately I needed. You're a saint for handling the spiraling, self-doubt that cripples me sometimes. Thank you for continuing to show me I don't need to apologize for taking up space.

Thank you to Aurelia with Mayonaka Designs (@mayonaka.designs on Instagram) for the beautiful cover and formatting you did for this novella. I am so grateful for your willingness to continue to work with me.

To the Inner Circle - Jenny, Nikki, and Alyssa. Thank you for BETA reading and also handling my constant imposter syndrome. The posts and ideas you all come up with are amazing and I'm grateful you hold the fort down when I'm otherwise occupied. Thank you for operating things that intimidate me. Because this geriatric millennial just cannot.

To D. Raven's Unkindness - thank you for sticking with me through a chaotic debut and the suddenness of a Christmas novella. I am beyond grateful for the constant hype of my posts and support you all continue to give me. Thank you for loving my characters and books as much as I do and shouting it to the world. Lucas Marshall says you are all such good girls. *wink*

And to my readers, without you I wouldn't be continuing. I've been blown away by the love you all have given this baby indie author and pray you all love the following books just as much. Thank you for loving Thirteen Years and reading First Christmas.

ABOUT THE AUTHOR

D. Raven is a single mom of one special needs child. She lives in the Midwest portion of the United States.

Being unable to work due to her child's needs she relies on the kindness of her family and friends a lot. In order to try to earn income herself and pursue a lifelong passion, she started writing

She loves reading, writing, music, and friends. She is a fierce introvert.

You can find her on Instagram, Amazon, and Goodreads.
IG: @author_d_raven
Email: Draven.writesromance@gmail.com
Goodreads: Author D. Raven
Website: www.dravenbooks.com

Her books' Spotify playlists can be found on Spotify at Author_D_Raven

Follow her for more updates and special announcements.

www.ingramcontent.com/pod-product-compliance
Lightning Source LLC
Chambersburg PA
CBHW070425310726
48977CB00003B/844